JOURNEY TO
REDEMPTION

Additional Titles by D Dean Boom
Fortress of Angels (2014)
See www.ddeanboom.com for more titles

JOURNEY TO REDEMPTION

D Dean Boom

Published by Mostly Normal Publishing, Portland Oregon
First Edition, 2015

Journey to Redemption © 2015 D Dean Boom

Map of Holimoren(detail) by D Dean Boom, used with permission.

Library of Congress Control Number: 2015907883
Mostly Normal Publishing, Portland, Oregon
ISBN-13: 9780692448557 (Mostly Normal Publishing)
ISBN: 0692448551

In memory of Brandon.

To my family—thanks, as always,
for all your love and support.

GRYPHILIX'S MAP

THE FREE CITY OF HOLIN

GULCH

EAGLE'S GLEN

MAGRICAN

REDEMPTION

ONE

Rainmaker

The hardest thing to find is the simplest: the truth.
—Elader the Old

A gentle rain fell over the farmland that ringed the sprawling city of Holin. Dar walked tall—as tall as his six straight days of hiking would let him. He focused on the city gate a quarter mile ahead and remembered the last time he had been here, some four years ago. It had been dark times for Holin then but a new time for him. That had been during his first training mission as a Journeyman, and hopefully things were better now. It seemed a good sign, surely, that the road wasn't lined with the dead and dying like before. The winter wheat, just shoots right now, gave the outlying land the look of unshaven stubble. The land looked healthy. Before long, he got to the gate and read its famous welcome: *Now entering the Free City of Holin. You are welcome, and you are now free.*

The road shifted from packed dirt to cobblestones, but Dar's elven boots still made no sound as he plodded into the heart of the city. He had a lot more magic with him now, and he knew how to use it. He passed several groups of troops, their armor shining and clean, as if it had never been used. Their presence on a street corner seemed to be keeping things quiet, due either to the threat of their menacing-looking weapons or their equally menacing demeanor—Dar wasn't sure. *Peace and freedom aren't free*, Dar said to himself, and he pressed onward. A few minutes of slow walking and he reached the best inn in Holin. He opened the heavy door and peered inside. Under new ownership, the place had both a new decor and a new sense of something he hadn't seen or felt in a while: hope.

"I need a room, keeper," Dar said as he walked up to the bar. Being fairly early in the day, it was empty except for the lanky man minding the place. Dar didn't recognize him. The old owner was short and round, almost spherical, really. If this was the owner, he was nearly the exact opposite to the previous one.

"I'll need the money up front," the barkeep replied. While the looks might have changed, the attitude remained the same. "Five gryphons a day. Prefer it in silver, no gems or jewelry or magical items. Food tab is separate, but if you pay four days' room in advance, I can put up a tab for drink and remove the cost from that of the extra days."

"Here you go." Dar placed five gold crown pieces on the bar. "No questions, no troubles—five days plus food."

Dar fought a smile as the barkeep stared down at the money. That was five times the amount he was asking for. Dar waited for the man's confused reply.

"You want five rooms, sir?" He realized he was staring and lifted his gaze.

"Just one." Dar looked him in the eye. "Plus beverage, plus peace and quiet."

The barkeep's eyebrows shifted from amazed to curious. "Quiet, sir? I'll give you a room in the back and not sell the rooms next to it."

"Not necessary. You can sell what you need, but I wasn't here, and you don't know about my room."

He flashed Dar a quick wink. "Just a ghost you are, sir." The barkeep pointed to the stairs that led to the rooms. "They are all clean and all empty. Pick which you like, and I'll keep it until you're ready to leave."

"I'm heading up to my room now, and I'll be out in the morning." Dar paused to let that sink in. It was just a bit before lunch, but he was tired after such a long hike. "I'll pay a like amount if I am happy at the end of my stay." He looked the barkeep in the eye. "Understood?" He turned and walked away before the keeper could say anything.

As Dar started his way up the stairs, he could hear the barkeep as he whispered to himself, "Abso-bloody-lutely."

The rain was gone when the sun crawled over the edge of the Edsea and brought dawn to Holin. Dar was already up, conducting his morning meditations to keep his spells fresh in his mind. Good sleep was key to keeping the concentration necessary for magic. Dreams had eluded him, but they often did in places with this many people. Dar thought back to his training in Magrican. Most everyone had latent magical powers. This wild, unfocused natural energy created a hidden storm of magical energy that those trained in the magic arts could feel in their bones. That's why Magrican was out in the middle of the vast empty area near the Vast Desert, and it explained why Dar's old master lived out at the edge of the wild. The swirls and eddies in the magic combined with the noise of the daily hustle and bustle to make him tense. He finished with a brief round of stretching to loosen the muscles he would need in a battle, though hopefully there would be none of that today. He packed a few items but left his armor, sword, and the rest of his heavy gear in his room.

Finally ready for his day, he stepped out of his room, cast a quick spell on the door, and then gave the knob a quick turn. It resisted. He gave the door a good shove. Again resistance. Kneeling, he tried to slide his fingers under it. They didn't reach past the edge of the door. He stood, happy that his room was secure.

He spoke not a word as he cruised through those patrons who had gathered downstairs and out into the town. He knew exactly where he was going, and the walk to Tellmare Manor was fairly short. Dar hadn't been there for quite some time, but he remembered it well. When get got to the heavily armored door, he rang the bell. Without a sound the door opened, and a man dressed in servant's clothes appeared.

"Yes?" said the man, a tone of displeasure in his voice.

"I wish to see your master." Dar smiled but knew it wouldn't be returned.

"Many wish to see his lordship." The man's dour expression became a full frown. "What is your business?"

"Tellmare's first name is Tell. His last name is Maar. M-A-A-R. He put them together to make the name of the manor. And when his uncle became second in command of the Dark Army, he changed the spelling…"

The servant held up his hand. "And who is going to be visiting his lordship?"

"Tell him the moon will be eclipsing soon. He will know."

The servant tried to show no emotion at the statement, but a momentary scrunching of his brow betrayed what he thought of the statement. He walked off, leaving Dar to wait at the door.

Dar looked around the outside of the house, lost in thought. Tell was an old friend, and they had fought alongside each other in many a battle.

"Dar!" An older man with short gray hair walked up to Dar, offering his hand. "How's it going, old man?"

"Hello, Tell." Dar took his hand and shook it with tempered strength. "How are you?"

"My back is sore still on occasion, but doing better." Tell rubbed where the rock from the Hill Giant they had battled had struck him, breaking many ribs. "If you hadn't had that healing staff, I'd have been off to the Heavens."

"You did the same for me many a time." Dar's half-elven body was still a long way from old age, unlike his human friend. His physical makeup allowed him to get into more trouble with fewer long-term side effects. "Have you been keeping up with your meditations?"

Tell's eyebrows lowered and a wry frown appeared where a smile had been. "In the city it's hard to cast spells, either druid or magical ones. Every damn time I do, I get five people asking me if I want to join their fool's quest—or some city ward asking if I want to join the Guard." He shrugged. "Either that or some youngling wants me to take him on as a pupil. If you can't learn anymore, how do you teach? You can't teach if you aren't still learning!" Tell raised his hands into the air, his fingers spread apart. He would start talking with his hands when he got mad. "But you aren't here for a social visit, are you?"

"I am still wandering." As Dar faced his mentor, a visible wave of sadness crossed Tell's face.

"Some never stop." He waved Dar in, and they each took a chair. "Until that boulder convinced me otherwise, I was heading that way myself."

A svelte woman, her belly bulging, waddled slowly around the corner. Her clothes fit too tight in some places and too loose in others. Dar could tell she was having troubles keeping her wardrobe up to speed as her body changed.

"Who is it, Tell?" As she spoke, the woman's hand went instinctively to her belly.

"Hello." Dar stood and offered his hand.

Tell went to her side. "You haven't met my wife. Allow me to introduce the lovely and once-pure Tharrah."

She elbowed Tell, who jumped back, grinning all the while.

"I see you're with child." Dar smiled. "Congratulations."

"Twins, actually." She rubbed her belly. "I'm due before the winter sets in hard."

Tell's face was barely able to contain his smug grin as he moved in close again. "As you can see, I doubt I'll be hitting the road again. At least not for some years, until my boys…"

"Or girls." Tharrah tugged at his elbow.

"Until *our children* are of age." Tell leaned toward his wife slightly and gave her a gentle squeeze.

Dar smiled warmly. They were very much in love—you could feel it as soon as they were within sight of each other. Dar smiled warmly, trying to hide a brief moment of jealousy.

"Sorry to intrude," Tharrah said to Dar, "but Thilson asked me about what your odd pronouncement might mean, and I knew that I had to meet you. However, I will bid you good day and take my leave."

Dar and Tell sat in silence until she was well out of earshot.

"She never asked me my name. She knows of the order?"

Tell beamed with pride for his wife. "She knows enough to not ask. She is a smart, wise, and powerful woman."

"And you love her with the whole of your soul," Dar said with a touch of longing.

"Is it that obvious?"

"Like the tracks of a rampaging dragon after a night of hard rain." Dar smiled at his mentor.

Tell laughed softly. Their eyes met. Dar could see that Tell wanted to provide some sage wisdom, but he had never been good with words. Dar paused to think about the challenge Tell most likely faced: How do you tell somebody who has seen just about every city and hamlet on this half of the continent that his destiny is still yet to be found out there on the road somewhere?

Tell cut to the chase. "You haven't said why you have come, Dar."

"I was in town." Dar looked away.

"I bet less than half a week ago, you were nowhere near here." Tell's eyes stayed locked on Dar.

"It was less than that." He looked at his friend. "And closer than that."

"Fabricate what you must to make your story work." Tell smiled at Dar.

"I can't stop feeling like I'm still just a student." Dar frowned.

"As much as you travel, you never feel like you've finished your training?"

Dar couldn't contain his fears any further. He blurted out, "How will I know I'm past my apprenticeship? How will I know I'm ready? I keep looking for challenges, but none seem worthy of my becoming a master."

Tell stroked his chin. "Maybe you're looking too hard. Maybe you need to let things find *you*."

"I suppose after, what, ten years now of looking for my destiny, it's her turn to look for me."

Tell let him think about his own comment for a moment before he asked, "What do you have to lose by staying in town for a bit? Holin tends to be an active place."

"I've wasted months on dumber things."

Tell's face broke into a large smile. "Like that time you chased that Fairy Dragon, only to find out he had been living in your knapsack since the first night of the quest to find him. How long did you chase him?"

"Two months," Dar said meekly.

Tell clearly couldn't contain himself anymore. He laughed from his belly, and it echoed into the whole house. "He really got the better of you that time, didn't he?"

"Being wise doesn't necessarily mean you know what you're doing."

"No matter how wise I get," Tell said, slapping him on the back, "I rarely have any idea what I'm doing."

Dar felt both better and worse as he walked back to the inn. He felt empty and alone, even as he walked through crowd streets. *How do you end up lonely in a crowd?* he wondered. He was caught up in his thoughts when a tall, heavyset man reached out to touch him on the shoulder.

"Sir? I need directions to the White Horse Inn."

It was the very same one he was staying at. "Ahead three blocks on the dawn side of the street."

"Thanks." The portly man walked off, a certain amount of urgency in his steps.

Dar paused and took a longer route. He checked twice to see if he was being followed and then subtly felt around for his gear. Once he was assured that he wasn't being tailed and hadn't been robbed, he headed to the inn.

The portly fellow was sitting at the table right next to the door when he walked in. Dar ignored him and scanned the room for troublemakers. The smell of stewing venison filled the air, with a hint of bread pudding chasing it around the room.

The serving girl unloaded a stein of some beverage from her tray to a patron next to Dar. "You stayin' for supper, sir? Bread puddin' and venison stew. The meat in the stew's so tender it falls apart just lookin' at it."

Dar considered it for a moment and looked around at the room, which didn't seem to have much in the line of unsavory types. There was a space free toward the back. "Sure." He pointed to the empty spot. "I'd like my dinner over there. With some water too, please." He placed a silver coin on her tray.

"Right away!" She smiled and headed back to the bar.

He went to his promised spot, a bench seat at a mostly full table, and sat down. Moments later two bowls arrived, and the steam wafted up to fill his nose with the aroma of the meal.

Eating iron rations, the long-shelf-life food of adventurers, for several years now made most real meals taste like manna from heaven.

Dar was four bites in when a man off to his left at the far end of the table pulled out a throwing ax and leveled it at a man at the end closest to him. The target saw the ax out of the corner of his eye and, being at the end of the bench, he tried to duck out of the way. Dar saw it too but, being in the middle of the bench, couldn't get out of the way and lowered his head to the table. He could feel the rush of air as the ax flew by. Dar got clear of the bench, stood, and turned to see the attacker.

"I'll see you rot in the Hells, you vermin scum!" The ax thrower pulled out a knife and rushed the target, who had yet to get to his feet.

"Please, no violence!" shouted the barkeep.

"Save me!" yelled the man as he struggled to get to his knees.

Dar pulled out the dagger strapped to his forearm under his shirt and sized up the situation. The attacker was smaller than he was and appeared to be armed only with the knife. But the pouch at his belt was concerning, and the knife appeared to have a liquid on it, perhaps poison.

This was an assassination attempt in progress.

Dar motioned with his hands and muttered a few words of magic.

The room went dark.

The serving girl screamed. A raucous buzzing noise, as if from a hive of giant, angry hornets, reverberated through-out the room. Suddenly, somebody dropped the mug in their hand—the sound of it shattering punctuated the wail of the bees—and then the sound of a body hitting the floor seemed to cause everything else to go silent.

The silence lasted a moment, and then light returned to the room.

Dar was now sitting, eating his stew. His dagger was back in its sheath, and he was blowing gently on his spoonful of meat.

"What the Hells just happened here?" The barkeep jumped over the bar and moved toward the two men on the floor.

One was starting to stand up, but the other was not moving. Blood slowly began to flow from underneath the man's midsection onto the floor of the bar. The barkeep went to the other fellow and rolled him over. His chest had taken multiple stabs from a small blade. Probably a dagger, and he was certainly dead already. What appeared to be the man's own knife was buried in his gut. The wounds in his chest were smaller than his knife, but no blade of that size could be seen.

"Nobody leaves until the Guard arrives." The barkeep walked to the door and opened it quickly. He pulled out a whistle on a chain from around his neck and made three long whistles followed by three short and finally three more long. He put the whistle and chain on the door, hanging it from a nail, and walked back in. He then turned his attention to the survivor.

"What's your name, stranger?"

"Drij."

"You got a last name?" He leaned in a little to help influence him to provide the information.

"I'll wait for the Guard, if you don't mind."

"Completely within your rights." The barkeep turned and stood by the door.

Dar just kept spooning in the stew as the murmur of conversation started echoing around the room. So much for the quiet.

It was several minutes later when a group of four guards came in. They were experienced adventurers, a look of resolution on their faces. One was dressed in plate armor, one in chain mail, one in banded mail, and the last was unarmored. Dar figured the unarmored one was a monk or magic user. The fellow in the plate mail took charge of the situation as the banded-mail-wearing guard took station at the door, making it clear that none could leave.

"Keeper!" the lead guard said. "You have summoned the Guard. My name is Strengstrick. On what matter do you need our attention?" He was looking at the dead man but still followed the protocol.

"This man was assaulted by the dead fellow." The barkeep pointed to Drij. "I asked him what his name was, and he invoked the Right of the Guard. I used the whistle, and you know the rest."

"Aye and thanks." Strengstrick faced Drij "What is your name, sir?"

"Drij. I will not waive my right to counsel."

"I will respect that right." The lead guard frowned. "What is your last name?"

"I will not waive my right to counsel." Drij crossed his arms.

"His last name is Bahara," came a voice from the corner. "I recognize him from the wanted poster at the square."

The man in the robe squinted at Drij. "It is so. I recognize him too."

Strengstrick reached down and started to draw his sword.

Drij spoke out first. "That is not necessary. I swear I won't hurt anybody again."

"True enough. At least not in Holin." Strengstrick turned to the fellow in the robes. "Brother, please place the seal on him."

The man in the robes started a spell, and as it worked, a blue halo formed on Drij. It finally disappeared as the spell was finished.

As the blue hue in the room faded, Strengstrick addressed the room. "Drij Bahara, you now have seventy-two hours to leave the Free City of Holin. You must leave the gates of the city and never return. If you do not leave, the spell magic will teleport you outside the gate in twelve hours. Should you return, the magic will trigger an alert at the gate, and you will be removed once again. There will not be a third removal. If you are found inside of the city after that, your life will be forfeit."

Drij collapsed to the floor. The guards paid him no mind.

"So, the dead man was attacking Drij. Did anybody see Drij pull a weapon on his attacker?" said the man in the plate armor.

"Sir, we didn't see anything," mumbled the barkeep. "Darkness fell just after the attacker threw an ax at Drij."

"A spell?" This piqued the attention of the man in the robes. "Must have been something like Darkness. Temporary and not continual. Unless it was dispelled. Then it could have been either. I could…"

"Where is the ax?" Strengstrick spoke with a terse tone.

The keeper shrugged.

Dar just sat at his meal, trying to avoid being part of the show. His stew was finished, and he was working on the pudding, taking the investigation in as it unfolded. One of the men, the one in the chain mail, came over and looked around for the ax. Since it was a key piece of evidence, Dar had known better than to do anything with it. The man in the chain mail found it on the floor next to the fireplace. He inspected it briefly before turning toward the man in the plate armor.

"It has fingerprints on it."

"Drij." Strengstrick placed his metal gauntlet gently on the man's shoulder. "Did you touch it?"

"No." He grimaced as he spoke and then shut his lips tight.

Strengstrick nodded at the man in the chain mail, who inspected the weapon and mumbled a few magic words. He closed his eyes and let the spell fill his mind's eye with a vision of those who had touched the ax. Dar had seen this before. It was a Recollection spell. A fairly minor magic, it would show the faces of whoever had touched the item to the person who cast the spell. Dar could imagine the dozens of faces that came before the guard's mind. Suddenly, he opened his eyes, breaking the spell. He looked around the room and then headed over to Dar. He stood over Dar for a moment as Dar kept eating his bread pudding. The man in the chain mail lifted up Dar's long hair and looked at his neck—noting, no doubt, the small sideways crescent mark.

Dar quickly turned his head, allowing his hair to drop. "That is an illegal search, and if you do it again, you'll have big problems."

The man in the plate armor fought off a smirk as he walked over to join them. "Well?" he said.

"Sir, this man just threatened a member of the Guard. I believe we should detain him."

"If you don't wish to be an ex-member of the Guard," Strengstrick, taking a step closer to the table where Dar sat, "I suggest you report out and apologize to the man."

"Among the dozens of people who touched the weapon, he's the only one here, besides the deceased." The look of the guard in the chain mail changed to disgust. "He bears the mark of the crescent moon."

"Right. So, at one point he touched the weapon, and he's a Journeyman." Strengstrick took a step closer to Dar. "Your kind is not welcome here. We can mete out our own justice. Myxil? Take a spectral image of the Journeyman."

The unarmored man came and cast a quick spell that made a perfect image of Dar appear on a vellum scroll.

Strengstrick resumed in a more haughty tone, "You also have seventy-two hours to leave the city. But unlike the felon, you will not be subject to automagical penalty for unauthorized reentry. Should you be caught and recognized in the city after those seventy-two hours..." He paused while a smirk built up across his face. "You will wish it was just a hundred of the Guard you were fighting."

He bowed toward the keeper and walked a few steps closer to the bar.

"I will consider this case closed for now. What happened is this: the dead man was trying to kill the one called Drij." He paused for effect. "And this attack was stopped by another assassin who was probably trying to kill Drij or at least capture him for some sort of reward." He looked around the room. "It is all but certain that Drij is going to be attacked again, so I suggest all innocent bystanders keep away until he leaves the city."

The man in plate armor walked toward the door and motioned to the man in chain mail. After a quick inspection, the body was picked up and the group ventured out in the waning daylight. The man in plate mail stopped at the door, the last of the group to exit.

"By order of law, keeper," he said, "if they are renting a room from you, you cannot forcibly remove these two until dawn of the morrow. At that point, I suggest you do so immediately. One is a target, and one is member of known shadow organization. Either is an issue—both is a disaster just waiting to occur."

The barkeep struggled to choke out a short acknowledgement.

The man in plate armor walked out the door. As the door was closing, the voice of one of his underlings floated into the room on the breeze of the oncoming night.

"This man was poisoned by this own weapon and bears the mark of the Blood Brotherhood."

"An assassin, just as I figured…" were the last words heard from the guard just as the door shut.

Everyone looked at Dar and Drij for several minutes in silence. As people started to get up and leave, Dar could see the fear and hate in their eyes. He looked to the barkeep. Even the barmaid had a distraught look on her once jovial face. Dar left a couple gold pieces to cover the loss of business and proceeded to his room for the evening, hoping to limit the damage to the inn.

When Dar awoke the next morning, he followed his normal routine and then came down with all his belongings with him. As he got to the bottom of the stairs, he noticed Drij was still in the spot he had collapsed in the night before.

"I'm, um," the keeper stammered as his eyes met Dar's.

"Keeper, please keep the remaining amount of the down payment for my room. I do not hold you responsible for my being forced out of Holin earlier than planned."

"Is it true?"

Dar had expected the barkeep to say something, but the words weren't his. Dar turned to look at Drij, who spoke the words again: "Is it true?"

"Is what true?" Dar's hand went to his sword hilt, mostly by instinct.

"Is it true that the Journeymen are agents of good, not evil and subversive like the legends would have us believe?"

Dar had answered this question before. He swept his free hand through the air to make his speech seem more grand. Something Tell had suggested years ago. "Some people think that to challenge the status quo is to be subversive. To ask why the weak suffer while the powerful do nothing is to some the most dangerous question. My brotherhood, the Journeymen, seeks only justice and fairness. I only fight went I have to, if that is what you mean."

Drij stood up. "How do you find people that need help?"

Dar's hand eased off the sword. He folded his arms across his chest. "Do you know someone who needs my help?"

"I now know what I must do." Drij looked down at the floor. "But I will need a guard to help me. As you saw last night, I'm a marked man. I cannot tell you the reasons, for I will not speak of the crime I have committed. But if you will help me get to the end of my journey, I will pay you handsomely."

Dar shifted his weight away from Drij. "I'm not the type that can be bought and paid for. I take jobs because they are interesting or help the less fortunate. This sounds like neither."

Drij extended his arms as if in prayer, and tears welled up in his eyes. "I'm a man without family, without country, without anything but my sins, and I need help to provide some closure to my disgrace. I want you to help me go to Redemption. I want to go there to be forgiven—" Drij gulped in a breath as a tear rolled down his cheek—"and then take my own life and die in peace."

Drij's words hung in the air like a cloud waiting to rain. Dar looked him in the eye and catalogued what he saw. No fear, no anger—just remorse, hurt, and suffering. Drij didn't look like he was afflicted with some ailment, unless his girth had become an impediment to his health. Underneath his surface emotions, there was love, touched with betrayal and a sense of finality that only great suffering could create.

Dar paused and reflected for a moment before speaking. "I'll take you to Redemption. But the fee you're offering must go to a charity."

"Except your expenses, I imagine." Drij frowned.

"If you're truly looking to be forgiven and go to the Heavens, I don't need your money. My reward for helping a soul in need will come later, in the afterlife."

"I respect that." Drij nodded. "So, what do we do now?"

"To get to Redemption, we'll need to travel over a thousand miles, and we have nothing but what we carry with us. We need to head to the outskirts of the town and look for the station of the coach wagon."

Dar nodded at the keeper and opened the door.

TWO

Forty-Six for Two

The journey of a thousand miles is most easily
completed with magic or a beast of burden. Or
better still, a magical beast of burden.
—*Alix Dee'lee's Traveler's Guide to Holimoren*

I t had rained overnight, and the cobbles were littered with
small pools and puddles. Dar walked briskly, forcing Drij to
jog at times to keep up.

"I didn't catch your name…" Drij blurted out between
pants and puffs.

"Dar Aurlyss. Should I call you Drij or Bahara?" Dar had
run into enough cultures that had the family name first that he
felt he should check.

It took Drij a second to answer. "Drij. I have disgraced
my family, and they don't need me as a burden anymore."

"Look," started Dar as he slowed down to allow Drij to
walk beside him, "if you don't want to talk about your incident, your crimes…that's fine. Just stop bringing it up."

Drij stopped, but Dar continued.

"Fair enough." Drij jogged again to catch up.

"Do you have any weapons?" Dar eyed his new partner in the dawn's light.

"No, nor do I want any. If I am to be killed, I will not defend myself."

"But you will dodge again, like in the inn, will you not?"

"That was instinct, nothing more." Drij upped the tempo of HIS stride slightly. "I wish to reach Redemption and make my peace before exiting this world for the next."

"So you say." Dar noticed the change in Drij's speed and modified his gate to match. "How much do you know of Redemption? Have you been there before?"

"I know what the legends say. And I had an uncle who traveled there with his wife when she was facing death."

"Did they make it?"

"No." Drij's voice took a somber tone. "She was buried alongside the road."

"Hopefully, we won't join her." Dar scanned the crowd ahead, looking for the landmark at which he knew to turn dawnside in order to get to their destination.

"How are we going to get there?"

The city clutter split open to reveal a large open space devoid of buildings. It was also lacking trees, but small tents and other temporary structures dotted the commons. Farther along the path was a large sign. It read *Gryphilix Bus and His Amazing Coach Wagon.* Behind the sign were two enormous six-legged reptiles, each at least fifteen feet long and six feet at the shoulder, pulling a wagon almost thirty feet long and easily ten feet at its tallest. A tall, pale man with leather armor the color of storming clouds sat at the reigns. He had white wings like an egret, and you could feel his gaze from across the distance. A small crowd of people, a mix of the infirm and their loved ones, had gathered at the back of the coach wagon, and it was clear that the odd collection of people and machinery was about to get under way.

"What is *that*?" Drij asked. Dar knew it was easy to have lived in Holin for decades and never seen this before. This was a service that only those who needed it could find. Or would want to.

"A marvel of modern technology and business sense," Dar replied, musing for a moment about what Drij's reaction would be to some of the more wild things he had seen.

"Your plan is for us to ride in it?"

Dar picked up the pace. "Unless you would like to walk a thousand miles to the center of Holimoren, yes."

Drij stopped. Dar kept going.

Without looking back, Dar said, "A thousand miles for a man your shape would be a near-impossible trek. This will be fast, safe, and give us good odds for getting you there alive."

Drij started jogging again, and he rapidly closed the gap. "Why not just get a magic user to teleport us—or some other magical means?"

Dar suddenly stopped, and Drij had to halt violently to avoid running him over.

Dar leaned in so his words had power without being loud. He looked at Drij with a fire in his eye. "Do you, as a marked man, want to go to a person who probably either works for the Guard or is a member of the Magic Guild with somebody who is in the Guard? Or is just a busybody who happens to see the wanted poster of you in the town square? You want to give somebody who would stand to profit from your being teleported back to wherever you did whatever you did an opportunity collect their reward? You said you needed to get to Redemption. You said you needed to get there without getting killed. This coach wagon provides us a low-attention means of doing so that meets all your requirements." Dar waved his arm toward the coach wagon. "Sure, it isn't gold plated, and the people in it are most likely sick and dying, but you're not long for this world anyway. We can do it your way, and you can be dead in minutes, or you can do it my way and have the time to do what you wish to do to prepare your soul for eternity."

Drij fell to his knees and closed his eyes as his lip began to tremble. He raised his hands to rub his head. "I'm just used to being the one in control, and now everything is moving so fast." Drij pleaded with his eyes. "Everything is changing, and I'm not used to it."

Dar looked sternly at Drij, his patience fading. The two remained motionless for what seemed like forever, until a whistle broke the silence

"You've had your time to think it over," Dar told him. "The coach wagon leaves in five minutes. It's a two-minute walk, and we have a few minutes of haggling to do before we can board. I suggest we resolve on a course of action and act on it."

Drij wiped the tears from his cheeks as he stood. "We'll be there in one minute, and I'll pay his price, no haggling. As you have pointed out, I won't need my money where I'm going." He started running to the back of the coach wagon. "It didn't bring me gain—might as well bring somebody else gain."

"Okay, then." Dar started to jog after him. "Let me do the talking and keep your head down."

"Fine," Drij said, panting already out of breath just a few steps into the sprint.

When they got to the back of the wagon, they approached the scrawny kid who appeared to be collecting the fares. As Dar broke his stride and stopped running, he spoke to the fare collector. "Two to Redemption, please."

"Fifteen gold each. Up front. In gold or platinum." The collector's tone told Dar this was a well-rehearsed speech. "No small coins, no jewelry. No gems. No magic items."

Dar reached into his pouch and pulled out six platinum coins. "Do I talk to you about getting a good seat?"

"That discussion is for Mr. Bus."

Dar put away his pouch. "It's still run by Gryphilix Bus, right?"

"Do you know him?" The lad seemed amused that somebody knew the boss.

"We'll see if he remembers me. I'll talk to him after we leave town."

"You'll need to do it before his first route-check flight."

"Thanks, you have been quite helpful..." Dar drew out the last part of the sentence."

"Bounce. They call me Bounce."

Dar smiled. "Okay, Bounce. Thanks for your help."

The two stepped up onto the small wooden bench that helped people into the coach wagon. Up close the wagon was more even more impressive than the last one Dar had been on. A metal understructure held the wooden monstrosity together, and the large wheels appeared to be made from some sort of black material. The lizards at the front were about the size of dragons but with six legs and long spikes running the length of their spines. There was a thin metal rod construct at the front, though it wasn't obvious what it did. It looked like a ship's boom—or like a crane boom—but there was nothing to hoist, and it wasn't large enough to lift much. The seats of the coach wagon were covered in cloth, and while worn, they looked soft enough. The wood of the driver's enclosure went up to a thin skin roof that extended over the whole wagon, though it looked like it would only keep the people inside dry if the wind didn't push the rain too much. Underneath the driver's area was a room, sealed to the elements. In the back corners were privy holes with curtains to provide some sort of privacy. The only seats free were right next to the one on the dawn side of the seating area.

"It will only be until we talk to Gryphilix," Dar assured Drij.

"I don't care," said Drij rather flatly.

Dar ignored Drij's reply. "Bounce?"

"Yeah?" The youth was still securing items as the wagon got moving.

"How many other people are on the coach wagon today?"

"Two short of four dozen."

"Is the Box empty?"

Bounce chuckled. "As always. Not many people pay extra. Those that can don't travel with this lot. Boss is out of his head if he thinks people will pay that much for it."

"How long until we leave?"

Another whistle blew a long, shrill note and the purpose of the boom was revealed. It hoisted a carcass of some medium-sized mammal from underneath the driver's seat and out in front of the lizards, just out of their reach. They started to walk after the food, but never got any closer to it. Finally, they ended up running. The boom was able to pivot in any direction, so steering was accomplished by moving the food in the direction you wanted to turn. Quick turns were not possible, but given the size and bulk of all the pieces involved in the coach wagon, all traffic either moved out of its way or was destroyed by it. Quickly the creatures reached full speed, which condensed almost a half-day's walk into just an hour. In no time flat, they were well clear of the city and on the open road.

Dar looked around at the various passengers huddled along the length of the seating area. He mentally catalogued several families and at least one pregnant woman, figuring them all to be human. None appeared to be immediately dangerous. He worked his way along the rail to the front of the coach and started to talk to the driver.

"Gryphilix Bus." Dar spoke over the noise of the wheels.

Gryphilix turned to face him. "Yes?"

"I'd like to arrange an upgrade to the Box."

"Should have bought it back in town." He stared at Dar, as if trying to read his soul.

"I changed my mind, and it's still empty." Dar kept his eyes locked on driver's.

"Now I recognize you. You're that unlucky fella."

Dar kept his hands steady on the ropes that lined the seating area. "Unlucky?" He tried to keep his face without a hint of emotion. But it wasn't working.

"Smirk at me all you like, but every time you are on board, it's trouble for me!"

"You consider people not dying bad luck?"

"These lizards don't feed themselves." Bus turned to focus on the pulleys. "A certain loss is required to keep the operation cost-effective."

"Look." Dar leaned closer so only they could hear. "I'll pay you the fee for the Box. I'll pay it for each person I put inside. Then you'll have enough money to feed your lizards and your greedy soul."

Gryphilix huffed and frowned. "I ain't greedy. You feed the lizards and pay the flat fee, and I'll let you put a devil in the Box if you want."

"Deal." Dar produced a small bag that clinked as he handed it over. "When you've satisfied yourself with the amount, you tell me, and I'll get the people into the Box."

"I can tell by the weight and the clink it is forty platinum coins." Gryphilix shook it gently. "And a couple of extras, like maybe a copper or two."

"Keep them." Dar watched as the rolling hills of the landscape went by.

"Move your people when you want." Gryphilix turned back to the lizards.

The Box was like a small house that sat behind the driver but above the main deck that housed the regular passengers. It was heated, sealed, and possessed both windows with curtains and a fair-sized bed, complete with extra cushions. It even had its own bathroom. It had two entrances, one from the main deck and the other a door that opened along the side. Dar walked back to the main deck and walked up to the man who was holding the hand of the pregnant woman. A small, dirty child huddled beside them. The woman was not well, and the child didn't look much better.

Dar said, "I have come to tell you that you can use the private room at the top of the coach."

"We can't afford that, sir." The man spoke barely above a whisper.

Dar rubbed the head of the child and mumbled something under his breath before looking up at the man. "It is taken care of."

The child started looking around. Slowly, the color in her cheeks came back.

"And let me help your wife to the Box," Dar continued. He turned to the child. "Go ahead, go to the front of the wagon."

The child ran off toward the entrance from the main deck, and Dar started to mumble again as he helped the woman toward the short stairs that led to the entrance. By the time they reached the opening, she was walking without any help and her color too had returned to normal. The pink of her cheeks shone like first light, and it made all who could see her face smile.

The man, seeing his wife and child feeling better, clearly also started to feel better.

"Enjoy." Dar turned to walk back to Drij.

"May the gods bless you, sir," said the man, with tears welling up in his eyes. "I wish I could pay…"

"Your child's smile and your tears have already paid any debt in full."

Dar motioned to Drij that they could take the spot the family had recently occupied on the main deck.

"You healed them, didn't you?" Drij asked.

"I did what was required." Dar sat down.

"Why didn't you put us into the Box?"

"We don't need it." Dar looked at Drij. "They did."

As Dar spoke to Drij, he could see back to where they had boarded the wagon. Bounce was there, observing the scene with the family unfold. Dar noted that there was something about what he had done that made Bounce look very unhappy. Without noticing Dar's eyes, Gryphilix's assistant reached up to the last flagpole and removed a red flag. Dar wondered about what that was about, but it would wait. He sat and let the miles go by.

Some time later Dar stopped meditating as he noticed Bounce walk past him and up to the front of the coach wagon. Dar stood up and watched as Bounce took over the reins. Gryphilix moved to the back near the stairs where everyone boarded and stretched, apparently making sure his wings were in good shape. He gave a quick test, floating just above the deck as Dar watched.

"Can I help you?" Gryphilix clearly didn't like being stared at.

"Just wondering what you're doing. You didn't do this last time."

"Just these last couple of months there have been ambushes set up at various points on the routes. I fly ahead and use my higher vantage point to root out the buggers and move the route every trip."

"And?"

"So far it has worked."

No sooner had Gryphilix finished than an arrow flew past his face and buried itself deep in the timber that held up the roof. Instinctively Dar turned and pulled his bow from around his chest. Unlike a normal bow, his started out as a sagging piece of wood made out of a willow tree, supple and able to conform to his body. This flexibility made it able to survive all but the hardest direct blows. As one arm swung the bow into position, the other quickly fetched an arrow from the quiver on his back. The bow started off floppy but quickly grew more and more rigid as he pulled on the string. Finally, as the bow reached full draw, it was as hard as a normal bow and Dar was ready to fire. He scanned the area, looking for a target.

"Over there!" Gryphilix yelled, pointing into the distance.

Out about fifty feet away was a pack of dire wolves with goblin riders. Two were putting away bows—Dar hadn't seen anymore arrows, which meant their aim was as bad as their smell. The rest were pulling out axes and spears and charging the coach wagon. Dar turned to face the lead rider and let fly his arrow.

"Everyone get down!" he yelled.

The goblin didn't see the inbound arrow until it reached his chest and penetrated his shoddy leather armor. Green blood immediately began oozing from the wound. Mentally marking that as a kill, Dar turned his attention to another goblin and drew another arrow from his quiver. Figuring the ones with spears to be the most dangerous, he picked the nearest rider with a spear and let another arrow fly. This time it missed as the wolf veered to the side. The whole pack was following suit, Dar quickly realized—probably looking to circle away from the arrow fire. When the first wolf turned, the rider fell off, an arrow sticking out of the center of his back.

"To arms! To arms!" Gryphilix was shouting again, but most of the people just huddled underneath the outer wooden edge of the coach wagon, looking for cover.

"It's just you, me, and Bounce. I hope you're a good fighter, Gryphilix."

"One of the best." Gryphilix jumped into the air and drew the morning star from his belt. The heavy ball pulled on the chain that held it to the long wooden handle in his hand—designed for swooping attacks, the ball had all the momentum and did all the damage. But since blades can get stuck, and stuck meant staying on the ground, Dar reasoned that Gryphilix must have liked his weapons blunt so they wouldn't limit his maneuverability. As he watched Gryphilix continue his climb into the sky, Dar noticed that Bounce wasn't at the controls anymore. Perhaps the second arrow hadn't missed?

"I need a count!" Dar called up from below.

"Ten worgs and nine goblins," came Gryphilix's reply.

Dar watched the horde as it wheeled around and started to come in at an angle that made archery ineffective. He still fired a bunch of arrows, but only one hit, in the hindquarter of the last worg, as Gryphilix called them. The arrow seemed to slow the creature just enough that it dropped behind slightly. Suddenly Gryphilix swooped down and crushed the head of the wolf with the morning star, and the goblin flew into the air as its momentum carried it forward. The goblin ended up underneath the dead heap of the wolf, and it was obvious the green-skinned monster had suffered severe trauma from the crash. Pinned under the wolf's weight, it quickly quit struggling and finally quit moving.

Back at the coach wagon, Dar quickly moved all the passengers to the side opposite the horde. As the range shortened, his bow became more effective, and another two riders and their mounts ended up dead. Just before the remaining six sets of attackers arrived, Gryphilix landed gently next to Dar.

"The last worg just left to eat one of his dead comrades. These aren't quality fighters, you know."

"It's not the quality that concerns me," Dar said, "it's the quantity. The wolves can't jump up here; they will have to come around the back." He was taking deep breaths; firing the bow rapidly was hard work.

"The worgs will probably go after the lizards." Gryphilix wasn't even winded yet..

"What will the lizards do?" Dar put his bow away.

Gryphilix ducked as a thrown hand ax sailed past his head and continued out of the wagon altogether. "Probably fight back. Maybe eat a couple."

"So you aren't worried?"

"Not a lick." He turned to Dar and smiled.

Dar pulled out his sword, and a light mist formed around the blade.

"Interesting," Gryphilix commented.

"Something we can talk about later," Dar promised as the first goblin came over the railing.

The goblin had a short sword with a slight curve. He was quickly joined by four more of his fellows bearing the same weapon. The last of the six had a short stick as his only weapon. They were spread out along the length of the wagon, the late comer being almost as far back from Dar as the Box.

"A wand!" Dar yelled. But it was too late. Gluey strands of webbing shot out of the wand and covered Gryphilix, pinning him to the roof and floor. Dar countered by pulling out his dagger and throwing it at the wand-bearing goblin. As the dagger flew, it started buzzing like a nest of angry bees. His aim was true, and the dagger hit the goblin square in the shoulder. But this goblin was tougher than the rest, apparently, because he turned the wand and pointed it at Dar.

Suddenly the dagger's handle turned into little wings, and the dagger flew out and plunged itself back into the body of the goblin—and then again and again, until the goblin collapsed.

The five remaining goblins charged him. Using his longer reach, Dar swung his misty blade in a wide arc and nearly beheaded the lead goblin. Frost cauterized the wound, and the goblin toppled, tripping the one behind him. Another wide swing cut into another foe, which again tripped the one behind him. This time the tripping led to the green vermin hitting his head on the floor, which appeared to knock him out. Dar parried a blow from the last standing goblin and ran him through, as the goblin's riposte wasn't fast enough to stop him. This goblin turned into solid ice as the tip of the blade appeared out his back, clear of its normal mist.

The two knocked-over goblins got to their feet and dashed to the back of the still speeding coach wagon. Turning to look at Dar, they whistled for their steeds. Dar's sword got to one before it could jump onto its mount, and it tumbled out onto the ground and quickly disappeared out of sight. The last made a clean getaway. Dar touched the dagger, which had returned to its scabbard on its own accord, but thought better of it and turned around.

"Well, you've got some nice toys," Gryphilix started.

"It's okay, folks, the danger is over," Dar said, brushing off the comment.

Dar froze the strands of the goblin's web with his sword and shattered them with a hit from the pommel. The look on Gryphilix face told Dar that he could feel the sub-zero temperatures the blade emitted as the thick sinews of web fell in fragments to the deck of the wagon.

"What is your ice sword called?"

"Winter." Dar rotated the blade slightly to allow it to glimmer in the light. "Your weapon?"

"Skullcrusher." Gryphilix lifted the morning star up to make the chain rattle.

Dar went to the front of the wagon where the goblin that had the wand lay dead and extracted the thin piece of wood from its hand. "Functional. I always went for more interesting names."

"So you named the bow too?" Gryphilix rubbed his wings as he asked.

"It came to me with a name. Weeper."

"From a weeping willow, I get it." The comment came from Drij. He had been nearby all the time but keeping out of harm's way. Dar handed him the wand.

"We could have used your help." Gryphilix sized Drij up as he spoke. "A man your size must have been useful at some point in his life."

"I was a priest warrior, until I joined the Holy." The urgency went out of his voice. "And then my prayers for spells quit being heard by the Gods and I lost the ability to do more than just wave a weapon about."

"Might I suggest that we save the talk for a time when the ticks and fleas from this vermin aren't spreading across the coach?" Dar nudged one of the goblin bodies with his foot.

"Wait!" started Gryphilix. "Let me stop the lizards first."

"Why?" said Drij.

Dar just shook his head, fearing what the answer might be.

"It's their suppertime now."

THREE

The Fire

Women are like fire. When handled with care,
they can bring warmth, pleasure, and bounty.
When handled recklessly, they can rage out of
control and punish and destroy even the hardiest
of souls.
—Elader the Old

Things were quiet until early the next day when the coach
wagon pulled into the small town of Elam. The lizards
stopped, and the coach wagon ground to a halt. Dar finished
his meditations, and Drij stood up—they had slept most of
the night on the hard wooden benches. Up front, Gryphilix
stretched his wings and jumped down onto the soft earth
to help set up for the passengers unloading. From the back,
Bounce set out the step stool and rubbed his neck. Dar stood
and started stretching as the door to the Box opened. The
members of the family emerged, each with newfound energy

and a glow about them. As the other passengers slowly worked their way out the back, the father approached Dar.

"You have no idea what blessings you have given my family. My wife slept all night, for the first time in ages, and when she awoke the baby was kicking for the first time in many a week."

Dar took the man's outstretched hand and shook it firmly. "I only did what was needed."

"Thanks," said the mother as she leaned forward and kissed him on the check. Dar reached out and patted her belly. As his hand lingered for a moment, the baby inside kicked. Her face glowed with renewed vigor as she continued, "I think the baby is thanking you too."

"A pleasure, my lady." Dar bowed gently. "Blessings always to you and yours."

The father worked his way back to Gryphilix as Drij looked on.

"Sir? Mr. Bus?" He started tentatively before become more forceful. "I would like to inform you that my family and I are exiting the coach and will not be returning. We are returning to Holin and will not be traveling to…"

"No refunds!" Gryphilix interjected.

"None wanted, sir." He held his head high. "We will find our own way back."

They started to wander off into the small town when Drij bolted from his seat, jumped off the wagon, and suddenly went after them. Before Dar could do anything, Drij reached the man, just a few feet away from the wagon. Dar considered pulling Weeper, but he followed after close enough to hear what was going on.

"Sir! Sir!"

The man turned to see what was going on.

"You'll need this." Drij held out the wand that the goblin had used. "You can sell it for money to get back to Holin with."

"What is it?" The man wrinkled his brow and looked at the wand like it might explode.

"It is a magic wand. A wand of webs—the command word is in goblin, and it's probably *web* or *shoot* or something like that. It should fetch more than enough to get you home in style. Perhaps you can trade it to a magic user for a spell ride back."

"You're very kind, Mr...." The man took the wand.

"My name isn't important." Drij held his head high. "The wand should fetch over two thousand. Use the money to keep your family healthy. Money is a curse without love."

"I will." The man looked at the wand, apparently trying to understand how something so small could demand such a price.

Drij walked back toward Dar, smiling. As he got close to the coach wagon, Dar caught the gaze of Bounce, whose eyes were aflame in rage. When Bounce noticed Dar watching him, the young lad bolted for the other side of the wagon. Dar wanted to chase after him, but the look on Drij's face needed an acknowledgement.

"Impressive, Drij. You may be forgiven before you get to Redemption."

Dar's words seemed to lift Drij's mood even higher. "Like you said, sometimes you do what is right because it is the right thing to do. We didn't need that wand. They did."

"Well said."

Both turned as Gryphilix walked up. "Gentlemen, we will be leaving in just about one hour. You're welcome to walk around the town, but listen for the whistle. If it blows twice, we will leave without you."

"I understand," Dar said softly.

Mr. Bus leaned in close and lowered his voice. "May I ask a question of you?"

Dar nodded.

"I spent all night wondering about your blade. A blade like yours has many amazing powers; it must have an equally amazing story behind it. Pray tell me all about it."

Dar wondered for a minute how much he should tell him. He decided that to earn trust, you must give trust. "It was made by an ice wizard. It is amazingly sharp, and it freezes its victims. It can also throw a cone of cold and will put out any fire. But it will also keep the temperature ten feet around me above freezing as it absorbs the chill to recharge itself."

"An amazing piece of weaponry" Gryphilix patted Dar on the back, a little hard for Dar's taste, but the sentiment behind it was genuine. "I appreciate your putting your faith in me by telling me about it" He lowered his voice even lower to make sure the secret was for Dar's ears alone. "By the way, the next town isn't for a couple of days, so we will be stopping en route for sleep. This is a most dangerous time. Can I trust you to help?"

Without a moment of pause, Dar nodded, and a smiling Gryphilix walked off.

After he was sure Gryphilix was out of earshot, Drij spoke. "Bounce seemed awfully upset by something today."

"I noticed it too." Dar's eyes darted around, looking to see what trouble the town of Elam could produce. His attention immediately focused on two women who were approaching Gryphilix. One was of medium height, probably five and half feet, dressed in a heavy white-and-black dress and carrying a large wooden box. The box was about two feet long, a foot wide but only about eight inches thick. It was made of a white wood, and while it looked pretty light, she carried it like it weighed a thousand pounds. The other woman was almost completely her opposite. She was tall, almost six and a half feet, with muscles on her muscles. Dar knew her kind. She was a she-warrior from the barbarian lands to the far north. She wore black leather armor and little else and had two short swords at her belt. Her hair was matted and unkempt, and her face was dotted with dirt. Each awaited her turn and spoke to Gryphilix before presenting him with a handful of coins.

"New travelers," Drij noted. "That she-warrior could be trouble."

"Actually, both could be trouble. We have no idea what is in the box. Potions, scrolls, maybe a weapon." Dar squinted a little at the box.

"A body…" Drij said in a knowing tone before trailing away. Dar turned and looked at him. "One day I will share my story," Drij said.

"But not today," Dar said for him. He didn't look at Drij; he was still trying to complete his assessment.

"Is that a request?" Drij glanced at Dar, apparently trying to read his intent.

"No, it's a statement. We need to get some supplies in town before the whistle blows."

When they'd returned from town with more travel rations (and some extra clothes for Drij), the two women had camped out their spots in the coach wagon and were settling in for the long journey. The she-warrior had little but her weapons, in the true warrior tradition. In addition to the white box, the other woman had a knapsack that they hadn't seen when she walked up. Dar settled Drij into a new spot and then walked over to the woman with the box.

"Hello." Dar left his hands at his sides and his body open and relaxed.

She looked up.

"My name is Dar."

"Not interested." The whistle blew once over the trailing edge of her statement.

"Come again?"

"Look, I don't want to sleep with you, I'm not a whore, and I am not carrying anything of value to you."

Dar took a small step back and crossed his arms.. "You misunderstand me."

"I'm sure I don't." Her tone was as icy as Dar's sword.

"Since we are going to be sharing this coach wagon for a couple of days at least, I thought we could be civil."

"Try the barbarian." She didn't even look at him as she spoke. The she-warrior turned at the sound of the derogatory term for her people but said nothing.

"If you need anything, madam," Dar told her, "I'm at your service."

"The only thing I need is space and to be alone. You're not providing me with either right now."

"As you wish." Dar gave a slight bow, frowning, but continued with his mission. He walked over to the she-warrior and tried again.

"Greetings, fellow warrior. My name is Dar, and my sword is Winter."

She stood and drew both of her short swords. Dar held his ground.

"Yspeida is my name." She held out the weapon in her right hand. "This, I named Hack." She held out her left hand. "This one is Slash."

Dar nodded as each was presented. "May we have the honor of fighting together against a horrible foe."

"And may all our weapons taste the blood of our enemies." She put the swords away. "You honor me with your treatment. It is hard to find dignity in this land."

The whistle blew twice in short succession, and the lizards started to pull the coach wagon. Dar wanted to check on Drij as they left, so he excused himself. "I wish to hear of your storied adventures, but I must check on my friend."

She sat back down. "We will have plenty of time."

The coach wagon quickly gained speed and left Elam far behind. Dar sat for awhile, keeping an eye on his fellow travelers. He paid special attention to Bounce, who sat in the back, apparently to keep an eye out for anything following them. Gryphilix rode high in the front, controlling the lizards, which needed an occasional course correction. Drij quickly got bored and fell asleep. So did the angry woman with the box, but she slept on the box. Yspeida stretched and shadowboxed and did push-ups and probably made everyone who watched her feel tired. The rest of the passengers did something in between what Drij and Yspeida did, but most went the Drij route.

After what seemed like an eternity, Gryphilix rang a bell, and Bounce headed to the front of the wagon. Bounce took over the reins, and Gryphilix went airborne. Dar checked the sun. It had been only an hour since they left Elam. He got up and walked around the passenger deck, searching the horizon, scanning the briars and thickets for trouble. Finally, Gryphilix came back and relieved Bounce. The coach wagon shifted slightly as the lizards moved a bit to their left. Dar went up front and queried Gryphilix.

"Something up ahead?"

"Yeah." Dar could tell Gryphilix was not happy by the look on his face.

"You going to share?" Dar started to look around even more. "Should I get Weeper ready again?"

Gryphilix turned and snapped, "I missed the first adjustment turn, and now I gotta figure out how to get us back on course, all right?" He turned back to the road and continued, "If it had been dangerous, I'd have left Bounce in charge and come back to tell you."

Dar nodded and walked back to Drij, who was now snoring loudly enough to stir the angry woman. Dar elbowed Drij, who quit snoring. The angry woman put her head back on her box and tried to go back to sleep.

Dar sat for a while but then felt the need to look around again. This time he walked back to Bounce, who was stretching his neck out after sitting at the controls for a while.

"Help you with something, sir?" the lad asked.

"So, what kind of name is Bounce?"

"A handle, really, if you don't mind."

"Really." Dar smiled at his honesty. "What is your real name?"

"Don't know."

Dar's smile disappeared.

"At the orphanage, we always just had nicknames."

"I'm sorry."

Dar couldn't tell if Bounce looked offended or bored. "Why? A rose by any other name would still be a pretty flower. Heard that from somebody once. But they said it better than I remember it."

"If you don't mind me asking, why do you run with Gryphilix?"

"Mr. Bus? He's a good fellow, and I needed to, um…" The boy's honesty seemed to be fading.

"Skip town in a hurry?" Dar knew the feeling.

"Yeah." Something approaching a smile appeared. "And since I couldn't pay, he let me work it off."

"Why is there a red flag on that pole?" Dar glanced at it to indicate which one he was talking about.

Bounce blushed. "It's how I dry my laundry."

Dar nodded and smiled. Then he returned to his seat.

And there he sat as the day went on and on. Gryphilix went back on his scouting mission twice more, and each of the passengers did as they felt compelled to do throughout the day. Boredom claimed each in turn, and Dar did some extra stretching and meditating to keep himself awake. Finally, the sun began to set on the far side of Holimoren, and twilight made driving farther out in the country dangerous. The roads from Holin to Elam were nice and wide, but out here in the wilderness, traveling at speed at night was a recipe for disaster.

"Night stop, folks. All out of the coach wagon, please."

Dar stood and looked around as the lizards finally crawled to a halt. Gryphilix said nothing for a few moments, apparently absorbed in helping the customers out of the coach wagon.

Each started setting up a lean-to or tent, and those that didn't have a shelter camped out under the coach wagon itself.

Gryphilix turned, and it seemed to Dar from where he stood at the side of the coach that he was going to hit Bounce. Instead, he said, "We need to set up dinner. You're in charge of the fire tonight."

Bounce smiled and started working the flints to get a supper fire burning.

"Driver!" Yspeida walked up to Gryphilix and drew both of her swords. "I offer you my services on a quick patrol and then the late watch."

"You're not familiar with my people, are you?" he said with a smirk.

She grunted a negative.

"We sleep once a month for four days. My next sleep is still a dozen days away."

She seemed deflated.

"But if you want to scout around, go ahead. If you bring back some carrion for the lizards, I'm sure they will appreciate it."

"Carrion! You can't fight the dead!" She put away both weapons and started back to the blanket that served as her campsite.

"They'll go faster too," he said loudly so she could hear.

"Then I will do it" was all Dar heard as she ran out of sight.

Dar set up a small campsite from the supplies in his knapsack for Drij, who hadn't been out camping since he was about Bounce's age. Assured that Drij was safe in the small tent he provided, Dar decided to go out for a hike. Alone. He walked until he was out of sight of the coach wagon area, and then he reached into his backpack and pulled out a black cloth that was shaped like a small door.

Dar placed the door on the ground and spoke aloud the magic phrase. The door went from being small enough to fit, scrunched up, in the palm of his hand to being as large as a real door. Rather than spreading out onto the ground, it rose up like a door in a building, but without anything to open into. This was only an illusion, though. Dar opened it and went inside. A while later he came out carrying a shield, a sleeping roll, and a quiver full of fat-shafted arrows. He said another magic word, and the door shrank back down to its travel size. Before Dar could pick it up off the ground, he thought he saw Bounce running from a tree nearby to the area where the passengers were camping. Gryphilix's assistant picked up some branches off the ground and placed them in his sack, acting like he had noticed nothing.

By the time Dar got back to the camp, Bounce had already blended into the rest of the group and the fuel had been added to the bonfire in the center of the impromptu campground. Dar set his shield down next to Drij's tent and went over by the fire.

"Hello again," he said to the terse woman with the box. She had a small wooden bowl full of whatever Bounce had made them for dinner. Smelled like a stew.

"Hello," she said. Dar feared the ice in her tone would put out the fire.

"May I at least know your name? I'd rather not just call you 'angry woman' if we get attacked or something."

"My name is Adalia." She quit eating her food just long enough to shoot him an angry glance. "But if 'angry woman' works for you, you can use that too."

"Thank you for that bit of trust, Adalia." He nodded slightly. "I hope to earn more of it over the journey to come."

"Don't spend what little you have." She didn't even look at him. "And I hope you take rejection well, because you'll be seeing plenty of it."

"Good night." He turned and walked back over to Drij.

"Wow," Drij started, "I thought your sword was cold and icy, but she takes those words to a whole new level."

Dar turned and oriented himself to face her as he sat down. "She has been hurt, and pretty badly, it would seem. She will come around in her own time, and I'll be waiting to be her friend."

"You've been hurt too, haven't you?" Drij looked away from Dar and out through the fire.

"Haven't we all? We all bleed from our own little wounds." Dar dug out a small snack of venison jerky. "You have the story you do not share; she has her mystery box."

"True."

"If life was an open book, it would be pretty boring. The trick is to be open enough to let people see a little more than just the cover."

"Here comes a test for your theory." Drij pointed the chunk of iron bread he'd been eating out past the fire. It was Yspeida coming in, covered in blood. From the look of her armor, it wasn't hers. She continued into the campground as if she hadn't a care and sat down. She didn't even try to clean the blood off; she just sat down and started polishing and sharpening Hack and Slash.

Dar called out her, "Yspeida, what happened?"

"What do you mean?" She continued to sharpen Hack.

"You're covered in blood," Dar offered.

"Glorious, isn't it? A bear. Big one." She stopped to spit on the blade to give the whetstone a little lubrication. "A fine test of my abilities."

"Aren't you worried about the smell of the blood attracting monsters or animals?"

"On my return I saw lightning heading this way. The rain will clean everything." She spat again. "Anything else I can handle."

Dar stood up and walked over to her so he wouldn't have to talk so loud. "If I may ask, what brings a warrior like you so far south?"

She laughed. "Why would a wild woman leave the steppes and come to this rainy and cold land?" She turned serious. "I am taking the challenge."

"I didn't know that she-warriors could take the warrior challenge."

Another pause while she put Hack away and started work on Slash. "I am honored by your understanding of my people."

"I spent several seasons near the Torrents." He looked her straight in the eye. "But that was a time ago."

"I am hoping to be the first. I am third in line to the throne of my house, and I want to have the glory of being an honored warrior. The fact that I am a woman should not make any difference."

"So what is your quest? Is it gold for your house or to kill a hated enemy?"

"To kill a hated enemy." She matched the cadence of her speech to that of her sharpening so she could be heard between strokes.

"Who, might I ask?" Dar had to speak louder to make sure he was heard over the sound of stone on steel.

She froze, her eyes locked onto the fire. "Our house was attacked by a single raider in the night. He snuck into the house and killed the pregnant wife of my brother. The first in line of the throne. He didn't just kill her; he cut open her belly and took out the unborn. My family tried to stop the attacker, but powerful magic was being used, too much for my people. They only were able to get the body back."

Dar joined her in staring at the flames. "I'm sorry."

"As the bastard left, he said that he would be back and he would bring his Journeymen brothers with him."

"Really." Dar tried to not show any emotion.

"And that day I swore I would not just kill one Journeyman, I would kill them all."

"How many do you think there are?" Dar swallowed hard. He hoped she didn't notice.

She started up the whetstone work again. "I know they meet in a large gathering around the time of an eclipse. There I will see them all, and one by one I will kill them. I remember faces forever. Once I have seen them, they enter my mind and do not leave. First I will kill the evil one who defiled my family. Then I will kill his family, one by one. I have sworn so, and I will die before I fail."

"So what if this defiler is not at that meeting?" Dar kept his tone flat, disinterested.

She stopped working the whetstone and looked at him with a questioning face. "He will be there. I have faith in that, as much as I have faith that the sun will rise."

"And if you meet him before the larger gathering?" Dar looked at her.

"I will follow him so he can betray his brethren. Then I will split him open and show him his own heart. Then I will..." She trailed off into a smile. "Do other things."

"I can imagine."

"You'd better not." She started working the whetstone again. "You will sleep better."

FOUR

Sour Times

"Needs must."
—Jean the Great

The night passed without much commotion save a cleansing rain. Dawn came and turned the sky a radiant blue. Dar conducted his meditations and spell preparations onboard the coach wagon. The hard wood benches were not the best for his exercises, but conducting them there was better than not conducting them at all. The healing spells had taken a lot of his magic energy, and only now was it returning to him. Drij sat and watched Dar—almost jealously, it seemed. Finally he broke the silence.

"I used to have spells too, you know."

"Really." Dar came out of his final meditation and closed his book.

"I had clerical powers." He looked down and took on a sullen tone. "Until I started down a new road."

"I didn't know there was another road for theocracy spells."

The words exploded out of Drij. "I fell under the sway of the Holy." He took a breath, which seemed to help him get his emotions under control. "Since then, I can only do the minor magicks. I have been forsaken by the gods and can't access the higher-power spells." The emotions came back, and he struggled to finish his thought. "After a while, I quit trying even the minor spells."

"So, have you been forsaken, or were you the one doing the forsaking?" Dar looked him straight in the eye.

"The father of the Holy promised full powers commensurate with the abilities we'd shown in worshipping the old gods. He said the new gods would enable us to use higher powers if we fully believed."

"And did you?" Dar kept his voice low.

Drij looked into thin air and furrowed his eyebrows. "I thought I did. I started having dreams—one of the new gods would visit me while I slept. And then it happened."

"It?" Dar tried to sound nonjudgmental.

Drij sat up straight and placed his hands on his lap. "Never mind." He stood up. "I distracted you from your studies. I should let you get back to them."

Dar looked at him. "When you're ready, I will listen. I will not judge, but you must be ready first."

Drij met his eyes. "I promise, when I can, I will."

The two sat in silence from the moment the coach started to move until just before lunch, when the wagon began to slow down. Off in the distance, a small town loomed. It appeared to be a small hamlet. The houses were thatch, and livestock wandered the fenceless town. It seemed empty.

At this hour one would expect children out playing, wives hanging laundry to dry, and men working hard in the field, but none were to be seen. All the chimneys were belching smoke, though it was a sunny, warm day. A hint of garlic and rosemary wafted in the air, making the town smell more like a meal than a sleepy little hamlet. All of which was not a good sign.

Drij must have read his expression. "What?" He looked concerned.

Dar reached under the bench and grabbed his shield. He studied the inside of it for a while before looking up. "I didn't think we'd be going to this town."

"*This* town?" Drij furrowed his brow.

"Eagles Glen." Dar couldn't hide his distaste.

"Rough town." Drij's tone matched his own.

"You have no idea. And the burning of garlic and rosemary means a great evil is nearby."

"A great evil? You mean greater than the normal evil of Eagles Glen?"

A smile fought its way to Dar's lips. "Yes."

Drij pressed his advantage. "You know, I always thought that Eagles Glen was a great name for a peaceful, fun-loving town. You can imagine my surprise when it turned out to be where the last remnants of the Dark Army decided to stop and wait for the return of their lord."

"Just like how Near is at the far end of the continent." Dar scanned the houses and trees for attackers.

"Exactly!"

"You know, towns change. Eagles Glen is almost reasonable these days. Hate and violence don't attract much economic growth. Evil isn't exactly a sustainable-growth business."

Drij started looking around as well. "True. It's sort of a pyramid scheme where it's good to be at the top but being at the bottom means a lot of work for few rewards."

"Sounds like you're familiar with it." Dar shot him a glance.

A pained look crossed his face. "I am starting to think I am."

Dar walked up to the front of the wagon with Drij following behind, apparently hoping to be included (or at least able to hear the conversation between Dar and Gryphilix).

"Why are we stopping here?" Dar asked him.

"Evil folk have money too, you know." Gryphilix chuckled. "Some even like to go places and do non-evil things."

"How long are we going to be in town?"

"Ten minutes, maybe less." Gryphilix's tone had turned serious.

"I'm pleased to offer my services as a guard during this stop." Dar made his tone match the driver's.

Gryphilix looked at Dar for a moment. His stern gaze appeared to soften slightly. "People here know the drill. It's mostly down-on-their-luck types who are trying to leave town after failed quests to slay evil—or it's ego-charged evil trying to leave on fair terms to go on a quest elsewhere. Either way I've had very little trouble."

Drij piped in, "Most of the people onboard are probably too poor to be worth stealing from."

Gryphilix nodded. "There's that too."

Drij continued, "Plus, I imagine that Mr. Bus's presence is a strong deterrent."

Dar looked at Drij and then Gryphilix, not fully convinced, "Very true, but explain the burning of the savior mix."

Gryphilix flared his nostrils and narrowed his eyes a bit. "Probably nothing." He worked the pulley, and the lizards came to a stop. "But I'll take your help."

No sooner had Bounce set the step stool down than a tall blond woman with hair that flowed to the middle of her back stepped on it and up into the coach wagon. Dar could see that she was very attractive, though much of her body was hidden underneath a heavy cloak.

"I will pay full fare, as long as we leave quickly."

"Aye, miss." Bounce nodded as he lifted her luggage into the storage area.

Dar and Drij worked their way over to her as she said, "Also, boy, I'd like the cabin, if I could."

"It is available, my lady." Bounce's voice seemed to Dar to have an oddly familiar tone to it. "It is all the way forward and has its own doors, both to the main cabin as well as out directly, my lady."

"Excellent." She threw him a bag that rattled like it was full of coins. "Take what is needed and then bring me the rest in my cabin once we are underway. I want out of this hell and its darkness right now."

When she started forward, her eye met Dar's. She stopped and offered her hand. "Hello. My name is Vulia. What is yours?"

Dar took the hand and brought it to his lips but did not kiss it. "Dar, my lady."

Her blue eyes seemed to be trying to see into his soul, but he did not wilt under her gaze. Her eyes held no affection or attraction—it was more intense, like anger, but at the same time, somehow, it was almost friendly.

"Well, Dar, I look forward to turning our acquaintance into friendship."

Dar let go of her hand, and she withdrew it back to her side. "As do I."

She glanced at Drij but looked away before their eyes met. "Excuse me; I have to get away from this horrible town. I'll see you later." And with that she withdrew to the Box.

Both men stood in silence until the coach wagon got back under way.

Drij was the first to speak. "Her voice has a very familiar tone to it."

"Somebody related to the incident of which you do not speak?"

"Not directly." He let out a deep sigh. "I am the only survivor of that." Drij went back to their bench spot and sat down. "But it is of that time frame, I wager."

Dar looked at the door, wondering. "When you figure it out, let me know."

They had barely left the Eagles Glen area when Bounce walked through the wagon and up to the door of the Box. He was tossing up and catching the little sack of coins Vulia had given him. It seemed to be lighter now by the way it was moving, but only Bounce knew the true story. He pause at the door and knocked. The door eased open a little, and he went inside.

Dar sat down, turned his gaze toward the room, and started counting in his head.

He quit counting after six hundred.

After what must have been twenty minutes, Bounce came out. His hair was mussed up, and his shirt was on backward. He silently walked back to his station at the back of the coach wagon; it appeared as if he was trying (and failing) to hide a smug-looking grin.

"Interesting," Dar said to Drij.

"That's not the word I would use, but it will do," Drij replied.

Vulia didn't reappear until almost an hour after they had left Eagles Glen. Her appearance was immaculate—it seemed like no hair was out of place. She was wearing a blue dress that went to the middle of her calf. Dar noted that while she had no apparent armor, the long sleeves of her garment could conceal braces of defense. She appeared to be only armed with her feminine guile, and Dar was at the ready for an assault.

She immediately came over to Dar and Drij and started a discussion. "Dar. What type of name is that?"

"Southern. Near Quinkalin and the Wall. What type of name is Vulia?"

"I'm from near Magrican..." She was sizing up Dar and ignoring Drij, who apparently decided to inject himself into the conversation.

"My name, Drij, is from the sunward approaches, near the Untamed Lands."

"Beautiful," Vulia replied without taking her eyes off of Dar.

"You are an adventurer, then?" Dar wanted to break up the uncomfortable moment, as Drij was starting to realize he wasn't invited to this conversation.

"What makes you say that?"

But it was Drij who answered. "Eagles Glen is known for three things," he said in an icy tone as he rose to his feet. "Whores, assassins, and foolhardy adventurers. So which is it?"

She finally turned and looked at Drij. "Why can't it be all three?" she said with a wicked smile.

"I believe his question is valid," Dar said softly. "If poorly worded."

She turned to face him, and her soft blond hair danced in the breeze from the open sides of the wagon. "He is very blunt, isn't he?"

The look on Dar's face told her she wasn't going to get a free pass on this one.

Her smile melted into an overly frumpy frown. "I am a rather defeated adventurer. I was in Eagles Glen after some money and some experience, and all I got was my spell book completely soaked on the first day and myself nearly killed the first night. I left the second day."

"So what was the town all in a panic about?" Dar asked.

"What do you mean?" she demurred.

"They were burning the savior mix, a supposed counter to great evil." Drij turned and went to sit down again.

"And you suppose I saw this great evil? I saw a bunch of orcs, and I fled back to town. Maybe they are part of a large horde, but without my spells, I was out of my league." She took a deep breath, then let it out slowly. This turned her expression from sullen to inquisitive. "Now, what can you tell me about the people on this thing?" Her gaze settled on Adalia. "What about her?"

"Angry. Travels with that box. Name is Adalia."

"And the barbarian woman?" She didn't look at the subject of her question.

"My name is Yspeida" came the voice of the barbarian from the other side of the coach wagon.

"And she has really good hearing," Dar finished.

Vulia walked away from Dar and over to Adalia. Dar sat and watched the conversation. It seemed pretty personable, but the tone was low and hard to hear over the noise of the wheels against the hard turf. Yspeida had tilted her head—it was clear that she was straining to listen in. Dar watched with interest as things suddenly took a turn for the worse: Vulia put her hand on the box, and Adalia jerked it violently back. The glare Adalia shot at Vulia was palpable, and Dar wasn't sure if he was going to have to intervene or not.

"Good day." Adalia spoke loud enough for the whole coach wagon to hear.

Both Dar and Yspeida stood up, slightly crouching, ready to spring.

Vulia said something that Dar couldn't hear.

"I said *good day*!" Adalia was on the verge of crying, and whatever Vulia had said wasn't helping any.

Yspeida started walking over to Adalia. Dar started too, but he wasn't sure if he was going to be stopping Vulia or Yspeida.

Suddenly Vulia turned away from Adalia and walked briskly up to the Box and went in. She shut the door slowly and appeared to be watching from the door as she shut it.

Yspeida slowed but continued to walk to Adalia. Dar was close enough now to hear her say, "Are you okay?"

"That witch wanted to know about my box." Adalia started to cry. "It's *my* box." Before long, she was sobbing uncontrollably, as if a huge flood of emotion had decided to exit her body all at once. "It's my baby…"

With that she collapsed. Yspeida just barely caught her before she hit her head on the wooden bench. Yspeida held her and rubbed her back and let her cry. Drij looked away—it seemed as if he was starting to tear up a little bit as well. Dar just looked off into the distance and tried to keep focused on everything going on around him. But when Adalia let out a moan that became a convulsive fit of tears, he could no longer take it and walked toward the stairs at the back of the coach where Bounce was watching the scene.

"Wow. She really blew up, didn't she?" Bounce's tone showed that he had never felt that kind of eviscerating pain before.

"That type of hurt runs deep," Dar said.

"What type of hurt is that, sir?" Dar was sure Bounce was looking to the Box, hopeful, rather than trying to understand Adalia's pain.

"I don't know, and frankly, I'm not sure I want to know." Dar stopped for a second and looked out behind him. They could still hear Adalia crying, but Dar did his best to focus on the journey ahead. "When are we stopping for the night?"

"Whenever and wherever the boss says." Bounce grabbed a pole and leaned out a little, looking around as he pivoted out. "I guess probably just a little farther. There is a good spot near here, if I remember right."

Dar looked at Bounce's "laundry" pole—thinking back, he hadn't seen much on it recently. "Do much laundry lately?"

"Ehh?" Bounce seemed to not know what the line of questioning was about.

"I haven't seen any more of your laundry on this pole lately."

Bounce's eyes widened a little and then darted around. He seemed to have nothing to say, but he was saved from having to think of something when a call came from Gryphilix.

"Bounce, prepare for encampment!"

"Sorry, sir," Bounce said to Dar, "duty calls!" He worked his way up to the front of the coach wagon.

Dar looked back at Yspeida. She was still tending to Adalia. It dawned on Dar that the look on the she-warrior's face could only mean that she too had cried like that and knew the pain and grief all too well. He knew some of the many she was mourning for. He contemplated for a moment. How many were mourned by Drij?

The depth of pain he had seen on the faces of Adalia and Yspeida hurt Dar down deep. When they stopped on a crest, he took a hike in the hills to clear his mind. It was a clear day, and the lack of clouds on the horizon foretold it would be a clear night, so Dar went looking for any signs of menace around the area. He caught wind of a skunk and spotted a bear on the other side of the valley down by a small brook, but otherwise saw nothing out of the ordinary. He sat down in the grass and started to meditate, which cleansed his mind as much as the hike had cleansed his body. Only after the stars had chased away the fading red hues of sunset did he get up from his repose and make haste back toward the encampment. After a walk of nearly an hour, he came to the base of the crest that the coach wagon had stopped on. In the middle of the valley but the highest local point, it was easily defendable and offered good sight lines in case they were attacked during the night. The coach wagon was especially vulnerable while stopped since it would take some time to get it moving again. At night the engines—the lizards—were sluggish, thanks to their cold blood.

As Dar scaled the crest, he looked skyward once again. He noted the mass of constellations visible across the sky, and lost himself for a moment in the Star River that dominated the heavens in an arc from horizon to horizon. His favorite was Ohryun, the half-elven hunter in the heavens, armed only with his shield and longsword. Ohryun protected the Seven Sisters from the unspeakable things that lurked in the darkest parts of the night sky—the places where the stars feared to go. Dar smiled has he noted how his life now had turned out like that of Ohryun.

But the smile faded quickly when he saw Adalia sitting next to the bonfire that Gryphilix had set up. She was alone, but her box was still within reach. Dar walked up as noisily as he could so he would not surprise her.

"I hear you," she said. Most of the anger was out of her voice.

"May I sit with you?" Dar came into the light, making sure she could see he had nothing in his hands..

"After I yelled at you, I'm not sure I deserve a friend right now." Her nose dripped, and she dabbed it with a small piece of white cloth.

"I believe you had your reasons. That didn't make it right, but I do understand." He sat down. "Well, as much as I can understand that much—"

"Don't say it, please; I don't want to cry anymore."

"Okay."

There was a pause while she dabbed her nose again. "I know I can trust you. I talked a long time with Yspeida. She said she trusted you with her life, and I figure after what she has been through, I could try trusting you a little."

"I am honored, and I hope to be worthy of that trust." As much as he wanted to touch her, reassure her, he didn't feel he had earned that right yet.

"Please just listen to my story," she said. "I won't be able to repeat it again tonight—or probably for another couple nights. And please don't tell the rest of the travelers."

"Why are you telling me?"

She gazed into the darkness, her eyes wide. "Telling Yspeida made me feel like I didn't have to carry the burden by myself. Once I tell you, then maybe…"

"There will be three of us carrying the load."

In the Box, Vulia rubbed the crystal ball she had just enlarged by using its command word. As she rubbed the center of the ball, it became hazy and then finally cleared. Inside the ball was an image of gaunt man. He was looking over a text when he realized that the magic the ball used was in his presence.

"Letin."

"Yes? Vulia, is that you?" He looked skyward.

"It is."

"What is the news?"

"I have found a vessel for our master." She was keeping her voice low.

"Will you be able to secure it?" His voice raised in the excitement of the moment.

"I won't have to."

Even through the mist of the crystal ball, she could see his frown. "How will we get it to the Lake of Tears so our master's soul can take control of it from his prison?"

"It is traveling there already." She smiled. "We just need to keep a low profile and take it once it gets there."

"You have duties associated with the Holy to attend to."

"I know." Her smile disappeared.

"I must see you." He narrowed his eyes. "I need." His mouth stayed open a moment. "I need you."

"I can meet you at the Curblack Forest near Hol Amroth."

"I will await your arrival." Was that a smirk? "Anything else?"

"There is another here who has been touched by the Master."

"Will he join our cause?" It was clear he was already thinking of their rendezvous.

"Yes." She started to rub the crystal ball, which caused the image to start to fade. "But probably not willingly."

"I really loved Trypia. And when he promised that we would be wed, I didn't fend off his advances. I believed we were already man and wife in our hearts, so I gave my body to him willingly. But once he found out I was with child, he left me." Adalia touched the cloth to her nose. "So I had to endure the shame of being with child without a husband or lover to help with its upbringing. So with just my mother, I gave birth. It was a hard labor, and the baby was late. Very late. For two days I labored, and finally the baby came out. I had already picked out a name, May, and I was ready to begin the journey of motherhood."

"But the baby was born still?" Dar said softly.

"As much as I cried and prayed and my mother sobbed and tried her methods, the baby didn't stir. And then as I lay in my bed, still bleeding from the birth, my heart still torn from the death of May, in walks Trypia."

Tears streamed down her face, but the firmness and strength of her voice didn't waver.

"He said he was happy to see that"—she paused—"'the problem,' as he called her"—she swallowed hard and then continued—"that had forced him away was taken care of. I couldn't believe he was there. I felt ill, and when I ran for the waste room, he blocked my path and told me he wanted me again now that I would be able to have fun again soon. I just vomited on him and collapsed."

She took out another cloth and dried her face.

"That was three days ago. My mother chased him out of house with a butcher's knife. As I lay on the floor, hoping for death so I could join my baby, it became clear to me, as if one of the goddesses had given me a vision. I felt in my heart, as if Our Lady of Compassion had said it herself, that I needed to bathe May in the purest place in all of Holimoren."

"The Lake of Tears in Redemption."

She shook her head and finished dabbing her eyes. "Our Lady said to me in the vision that the unborn babe will be given unto the Heavens if immersed in the water of truth while in the place of purity."

"So it isn't a box." Dar looked at the burden she was carrying with new eyes. "It's a casket."

"Made by my mother. Once May is set free, I know my heart can heal."

"You're a very brave woman," he whispered.

She started to cry again, and Dar wrapped his arm around her. There they stayed until the bonfire was just a flickering pile of smoldering ashes.

FIVE

Should Not Be

Every time I think I have seen the bottom of
humanity, I look around and I see that the bottom
keeps moving down.
—Sir Walter of Church Hill

When dawn rose, Adalia found herself tucked into a
warm set of sleeping blankets with May next to her.
This wasn't her bedroll, but she was a lot warmer than the air
at the tip of her nose. She looked around to see that a light
frost had dotted the encampment and most of her fellow travelers had moved right up against the bonfire. Gryphilix was
tending to the fire. When she last remembered, that same fire
had been just a small, dying flame.

"When Gryphilix figured it was going to frost, he moved
all the other travelers next to the bonfire and then he rebuilt
it." It was Dar, who was standing nearby, blowing onto his
cupped hands.

She sat up and went to peer under the blanket to see if she still had any clothes on. She had just opened it enough to see when Dar piped up.

"I put you in my bedroll, in your clothes." He kneeled down next to her. "I hope you don't mind, but I didn't think it was appropriate for me to do otherwise, and by the time Yspeida came back from hunting for the lizards, you were asleep."

"How am I so warm?"

He grinned and rubbed his hands on the tops of his arms. "A little something I picked up in my travels. It will keep you warm even on the most frigid of nights. I once slept in it near the summit of the Spire in winter."

"Magic?"

"The good kind." He smiled. "Too often magic is used to make weapons."

She nodded. "Magic does seem to cause a lot of suffering."

"Hungry?" He offered her a bowl of boiled oats.

"Yes." She realized she hadn't eaten since she left her mother's house. She took the bowl and started to slowly eat the hot and steamy mush. It was nearly without flavor, but she didn't mind. A full night's rest had given her an appetite, and for the first time in days, the dreams, the nightmares, had stayed away.

"Adalia, can I ask one question about your story?"

She nodded between bites.

"Every new mother that I have ever run into has been unable to leave her house this close to birthing, and here you are traveling and carrying a heavy load. How are you able?"

She left the empty spoon at the edge of the bowl and looked at Dar. "My mother is a powerful cleric, trained in the healing arts. She cured my bleeding and restored my body as much as she could. My body is as if I had never had carried the child at all."

"Amazing."

She looked away. "But my mother's own body was savaged by the effort."

"So that is why you are traveling alone."

She nodded as she spooned more oats into her mouth. Her deliberate pace had given way to near frenzy—she was suddenly so hungry. Had he had put some restorative elixir in it after Bounce had ladled the serving? She didn't care. She felt her energy and vitality returning.

Apparently, Dar felt a need to break the silence. "Once the lizards have warmed up, we will be on our way again."

The bowl was now empty. She set it down and started to climb out of Dar's bedroll. "Too bad they won't fit in your blanket."

Dar was helping to load the coach when a cry from Bounce broke the morning silence.

"Gryphilix!"

Dar rushed over to the lad. He was standing at the door of the Box, a look of fear on his face. As Dar approached, Bounce seemed more concerned than panicked.

"What's going on, Bounce?"

"She's gone!" He motioned into the Box. "The lady passenger is not here!"

Gryphilix and Drij arrived in the middle of his statement.

"That will do, Bounce." Gryphilix motioned with his hand that Bounce was to stop speaking so loud. "You'll frighten the other passengers." He waited a beat then pointed at the fire. "Make sure that is completely out. I'll deal with this."

Dar, Drij, and Gryphilix stood in the room and looked for clues as to what had happened to their latest passenger. After a bit Dar noticed that Gryphilix held a small, misshapen dagger. He was treating it like evidence, rather than trying to hold it like a weapon.

"I think a group of villains somehow entered and took her." Gryphilix looked concerned. It was clear that having well-heeled customers disappear wasn't good for business.

"I doubt it." Dar was near the bedding, and he could still smell her in the room.

"Well, Dar," began Drij, "if it wasn't some vile creature, what was it?"

"Not a group of orcs, at least. The door lock has marks like it was picked open by a thief. Orcs, goblins, trolls, and their ilk don't just pick the lock or knock and wait to be let in." Dar smiled at the absurd idea of orcs knocking. "They smash, they grab, and they destroy. They would have raped and killed her here. It would have been clear the moment we opened the door."

"I did find evidence of some sort of copulation on the sheets." Gryphilix pointed at the bed with the dagger.

Drij waved his hand. "Dar and I saw her 'entertaining' with—"

"Who, exactly, we won't name for now," Dar jumped in before Drij could say anything further. "And that probably accounts for that stain. Plus, if it was a horde of something evil, it wouldn't be *a* stain, it would be lots of them, and they would be bloody."

Gryphilix looked sick. "What are the other choices?"

Dar looked Gryphilix in the eye. "Maybe she just left?"

"Without my noticing?" Gryphilix looked around before coming back to Dar. "Maybe I just might grow another set of wings!"

Dar glanced at Drij, who said, "Maybe we should talk to Yspeida."

Yspeida was doing stretches and practicing her balance drills a short distance away from the coach when the three walked up. The lizards were starting to move about as the sun warmed them. Dar knew Gryphilix wouldn't want to spend long talking to her, but he wanted to make sure she wasn't blamed out of hand.

"Did you attack Vulia last night?" Gryphilix lifted his hand toward her, not realizing that the dagger was still it in.

Dar reached up and pulled the dagger down, as he could see Yspeida start to tense. "What Gryphilix meant to say"—Dar shot an angry look at Gryphilix and lowered his voice—"is, did you see anything interesting or unusual about the new passenger?"

"That whore? No." Yspeida looked down at the ground.

"Is that your word as a warrior?" Dar used his sternest voice and stared intently at her eyes.

It took a moment, but she looked up and met his eyes. "She had powerful magic. My people can sense magic, we don't…" She struggled to find the exact word she wanted to use. "Like…" Her face twisted up and then returned to normal. "Magic. I would have killed her while she slept if I had done anything." She looked back at the ground.

Dar's face softened as he figured out why she was so troubled by the questioning. "You could have killed her with her eyes open."

Drij caught Dar's lead. "I think she was more afraid of you than anything."

Yspeida's mouth slowly started to form a smirk. She nodded, a twinkle in her eye.

"We're done here, Gryphilix." Dar turned and started to walk back to the coach wagon. "The lizards are just about ready to run, and I bet you want to get back on track."

"You humans worry me," Gryphilix stated, shaking his head as he followed Dar. "You make no sense at all." He turned to face the lizards and looked to the sky. "Where did that questioning go wrong?"

Drij answered that one. "Dar made her reveal that she had been afraid. For her people, that is just as cowardly as from running from a battle."

Gryphilix furrowed his brow and reached up to scratch his chin. "My people have a saying: 'Fight and fly away and fight again another day.'"

"I bet her people wouldn't agree with that," Drij said bluntly.

"She would rather die than be shamed," Dar guessed. "Besides, my dear Gryphilix, doesn't legend say that your people were at the final battle of the War of Armageddon? Didn't they stay until the horrific end?"

Gryphilix pulled away a little bit—he was heading toward the lizards, and the other two were going to board at the back of the coach wagon. But then he stopped. "We were there." He shook his head. "But my people's histories make it clear that we were on the wrong side of that war, my boy. And we don't make the same mistake twice."

Before long, a fury of activity had gotten the wagon moving again. Dar felt better knowing that they were underway. His oath as a Journeyman meant he had to protect the whole group of travelers on the coach wagon, and that was a bigger burden than he could remember having had in some time. It was easier while they were moving. He rested his nerves for a while by sitting in the center of the coach wagon and just watching the land go by. The trees were changing from broad-leaved varieties that shed their leaves as the seasons moved on to trees with small, almost needlelike leaves that remained green all year. When he closed his eyes and took in a deep breath, he could sense the air becoming thinner. He could feel the coach wagon slowly climb the massive mountain at the center of the Holimoren. Most of the way up the mountain was their goal: Redemption. That mount was the Heaven Spire. Of course, most people just called it the Spire these days.

"Have you seen these types of trees before?" It was Adalia. She carried the small casket as always, but she was looking well.

"I have, many a time."

"Really?" She paused for a second. "Have you been to Redemption before?"

Dar smiled a sad smile. "Yes I have. Several times, as a matter of fact."

"Tell me about the first time."

"It's not a good story."

"What story about Redemption is a good story?"

"I'll spare you most of the details." He drew a deep breath. "I grew up with my mother in the lands of southern Frearea. My father and mother had separated just after I was born, and I didn't get to see him much. He had left Frearea in search of fortune and ended up mining coal near Hol Amroth." He ignored the looks of surprise. Hol Amroth, being at the edge of the Chaotic Disunion, was just about the complete opposite of Frearea. "The years went by and my mother, who was using magic to keep an eye on my father, sent me to a spot well east of Hol Amroth. She said I would learn why once there, and while I wasn't excited about such a journey with little explanation, I obeyed my mother." Dar shifted in his seat. The emotionally uncomfortable story was making him physically uncomfortable.

"At the assigned place, there was a man, fat and hunched over the horse that loped along the trail as if by its own accord. The man was pale and coughed when he wasn't wheezing for breaths that seemed to sap his energy. He was not long for this world."

Adalia meekly broke into his story. "It was your father, wasn't it?"

Dar nodded, keeping his eyes looking out in the distance. "What was left of him, at least. The mining had given him black lung, and rather than get it treated, he ignored it until it was clear he was it would take his life." Dar took in a deep breath and let it out slowly before he continued. "He wanted to see me before he died, but he needed to get to Redemption. He said he had to atone for his sins. Sins against my mother, against me, he.." A wave of emotions took the words out of him.

"It's okay." Adalia rubbed his arm.

"He never made it to Redemption. As I was getting water from a nearby stream, I turned and watched him collapse off of the horse, hitting the ground like a sack of potatoes. He was dead before he hit the ground. I guess the Gods couldn't wait for him to get to Redemption." He paused again to collect himself.

"I put my father on the horse, not easy given his size and my strength back then, and tried to keep going to Redemption. But he kept falling off, and I..." Dar needed another breath. "I couldn't get him to Redemption. I cremated him alongside the trail and took his ashes and rode into Redemption. I paid to have a dwarven burial crew inter him in a nice area. I was there for maybe two hours. I felt like I had failed my father, and being in Redemption reminded me of the pain his failures caused him. I rode home as fast as the horse would take me."

Dar patted Adalia's hand as it rested on his forearm. "So now you understand why I think Redemption is a beautiful and horrible place."

Adalia could only look at the ground. "I'm sorry about your loss. Was it a while ago?"

"You might say that." Dar took a deep breath and then promptly changed the subject. "Your question implies you have never left your own town. Is that so?"

She looked up, a brightness in her eyes. "My mother traveled a lot in her younger days, and when she had me, she settled down. In my eighteen years, I didn't want to see much. Then Trypia came to town and I..." She paused. "I just didn't have much reason to go anywhere until now. And Mother wouldn't let me anyway."

"I'm sure she just worried about you. But you turned out strong enough to take an epic journey."

"I hope I am strong enough." Adalia forced a weak smile.

"When I was your age, I could not have made this journey so quickly. I would have needed to prepare for years," Dar said with conviction. "What will you do when it is all over?"

"It will never be over." She stared out into the distance. "Part of me will always mourn for May. Even if I have a dozen children, she will forever be the one I lost."

Dar looked over at Drij. He could see that he was listening and something he had heard was haunting him too. His face was pensive like Adalia's. Drij caught Dar looking at him and averted his gaze, pretending to be interested in something in the distance. Dar thought he saw a tear, but when Adalia spoke he turned to look at her, acting like he hadn't noticed anything but her.

"I gather you've been all the way across Holimoren and back again?" Adalia was saying.

"Several times, actually," Dar replied. "I have been to the city of Near, on the great northern island of Bywater. I have seen the Edsea to the west, and the Narrows of the south. I have seen all points of the compass on this great continent. I have been inside the fortress walls of Magrican and survived a night in the vile town of Novassadra. There are only a couple of places I haven't been to in Holimoren, and one of them won't let me in."

"Like the Elvish lands?"

"Something like that..." He wondered if an ambiguous reply was better than a lie.

"Something like that? Being somewhere is like being with child." She smirked. "Either you are or you aren't. There is no maybe."

He folded his arms. "It's not a time I like to talk about."

She sat in silence for about a minute. "Well, I need to let you get back to your work." She rose awkwardly and grabbed May's box.

Dar reached for the hem of her dress and gave it gentle tug. "It's not that I don't want to tell you. I just need to know you can handle it." He lowered his voice. "But this isn't the time or place to figure that out." Dar looked sheepishly at her, hoping she would understand.

"If you want to be alone, just like a…a Journeyman, that is up to you." She pulled her dress free and went back over to her spot in the coach wagon. "Good day."

Even with his eyes averted, Dar felt Drij approach from the other side of the coach wagon and sit down next to him. Dar spoke without looking at him. "That didn't go very well, did it?"

"Love rarely does, in my experience." Drij adjusted himself closer to Dar so they could talk in soft tones. "At least during the early stages."

"Love?" Dar looked at him like he was a troll in a fancy dress.

Drij gave Dar a fatherly smile of support. "That is my estimation, but that is something you'll have to figure out for yourself. She has strong feelings for you, but she is tempering them because of the losses she has suffered and the times she has felt taken advantage of."

Dar let the words tumble around in his head. "You're awfully wise for an accused criminal on the run. What did you used to do?"

"Like I said, I used to be a cleric until I turned to the Holy and lost everything."

"I won't ask about the 'everything' part, but perhaps we should talk about this Holy that you mentioned."

Drij stood and motioned for Dar to follow him. They walked all the way to the back of the coach wagon and stood next to the exit. Bounce was driving while Gryphilix was out scouting, so this area was all theirs.

"The Order of the Holy, as they are called, is a new branch of the Conclave of the Gods. Their basic tenant is that the First Gods, as they are called, preceded the gods most mortals in Holimoren worship today. The First Gods, or the Holy, are the roots of the tree that yielded the entire pantheon that is currently in favor. Worshipping the original gods is supposed to lead to higher power and a true understanding."

"So you have forsaken the True Gods for these First Gods that the Holy preach about?"

Drij looked out at the passing landscape. "Not exactly. The Book of Truth tells that by worshipping the Holy, one does not renounce the new gods. If you talk to the parents, it doesn't mean you're affronting the children."

"If you believe there are children and parents."

"I do." Drij bunched up his face. "Well, I did."

"A crisis of faith?"

Drij's face became pained. "I lost all my abilities granted by the gods to the faithful."

"One set didn't grant you blessings because you had moved on, and your new lords didn't trust you enough to give you blessings?" Dar nodded as he spoke.

"Exactly. Well, at least that is what I thought. So when the Dreamweaver came to me one night and told me what I had to do…." Tears started to well up in the corner of his eyes, and he stopped.

"Do what?"

"I can't." Drij took a deep breath. "Not yet."

Dar could tell this was as far as he could go on that topic. So he picked another, and quickly so as to not cause Drij more pain. "So, what is the power structure of the Holy?"

"Power structure?"

Dar started to motion with his hands, outlining a triangle in the air. "What is the power structure? Who are the lay priests, and who is in control of the Holy? Who decides what the gospels are?"

Dar was glad to see the look of grief on Drij's face replaced by one of deep thought. "Our ideals are based on a tome called the Book of Truth. Our founder discovered it while fighting near the Spire. From there, the Holy was born."

"Have you seen the Book of Truth?" Dar worked at keeping his expression neutral. He had intended to ask about the book when it was first mentioned, so he was glad that Drij had brought it up again.

"Only the First is allowed to see it, and he keeps it with him at all times."

Dar looked Drij in the eye. "The First? Is that his rank or title?"

"I didn't ask, he didn't offer, and we address our founder only as 'the First.'" Drij stopped and looked off in the distance for a while, a frown on his face.

"What?" Dar broke the silence first.

"Nothing. I thought maybe Vulia sounded like the First, but that can't be. She is a she, and a mage, while the First, he was clearly a cleric."

"Maybe they are related?" Dar nudged Drij. "Plus, people can practice several professions, you know."

Drij laughed. "I doubt one can find time to become that high in the understandings of the gods and still find time to become powerful enough in the art of magicks that a she-warrior could feel the force of their magic."

"True." Dar raised his chin and then lowered it. "But it is possible."

Drij shrugged. "With the gods, anything is."

Dar took that as a sign he was pressing too hard and let it drop. After they had sat in silence for a while, he decided to refresh his mind and body. He started his stretches and his mediations, and Drij just watched. After a while, though, Dar noticed that Drij joined in with some stretches and meditations of his own, which he seemed to remember from his clerical days. The man's weight had declined rapidly during this journey, since the travel rations did little to encourage overeating—they weren't something you would be munching on because they were tasty. Plus, the extra exercise of keeping up with Dar seemed to be doing his body good.

Dar opened an eye and looked at Drij as he closed his eyes. Dar smiled, closed his eyes again, and went back to his routine.

The two of them were still going about it when they felt the coach wagon start to slow down. Dar wrapped up his meditations, stood, and headed to the front of the coach wagon to see what was going on. Drij, who seemed a bit sore after just those few stretches, caught up after a bit.

"What is going on?" Dar hadn't even noticed that Gryphilix had returned, but he was now back in control of the lizards.

The bird man didn't take his eyes off of road. "There is a fog coming down, and I need to set up camp at a good spot. This area is inhabited by Rock Trolls, and I want a good spot in case we need to fight."

"Rock Trolls?" Drij seemed to swallow a little bit harder than normal.

"They aren't that bad." Dar looked at Drij with a bit of a smirk. "If you hit them hard enough."

"We also have another passenger to take on," Gryphilix said. "I met her while flying around the area."

"She was flying?" Drij seemed to have recovered from the news of the Rock Trolls.

"Signaled from below with a smoke trail," he replied without a trace of excitement. Dar took his tone to mean he stopped for people like this more often than Dar would have guessed.

"And you stopped to talk to her?" Drij seemed aghast at the idea.

"She is only three feet tall. A halfling. I was not worried."

Dar jumped in to prevent Drij from saying something that might offend Gryphilix. "And she's going to join the coach wagon?"

"Paid double, plus a huge stopping fee." He turned and smiled. "My favorite kind of customer."

They stopped just short of the small rise. Gryphilix was aiming for the top, but the lizards decided to stop short—and when they stopped, they stopped. Gryphilix had Bounce set up the bonfire at the top of the rise, and everyone started their usual routine. They had just barely gotten dinner going when the short woman walked into camp. She was wearing outdoor gear—not too fancy, not too threadbare. Her hair was long for a halfling, silver with blond highlights. A sun-kissed tone to her skin showed she was not new to the outdoors. Gryphilix met her at the edge of the fire's light and talked to her for a moment before letting her pass. She settled down close enough to the fire to feel the heat but far enough away to not get in anybody's way. Dar watched her for a while, and their eyes met. They held the moment for a bit, and then each looked away. Drij watched from his vantage point but didn't say anything. Adalia occasionally glanced over at Dar, but she always turned away before his eyes met hers. Yspeida practiced her fighting moves and then got up to patrol the perimeter.

The members of the group watched and pondered each other in near silence until the fog came. The armed members of band agreed to take turns manning the watch, with Gryphilix taking the late-night shift.

As Dar took over near dawn, he caught Gryphilix as the bird man yawned.

"What was that?" Dar joked.

Gryphilix didn't smile. "The first signs of a much longer sleep than you're used to."

Off in the dark woods near Hol Amroth, Letin was waiting when Vulia flew in. She loved to fly; it was one of her favorite spells. Judging from the look on his face in the illumination of his light orb, Letin had been waiting a while. And growing more impatient each moment.

"Finally," he barked. She landed a few steps away, but he closed the distance.

"If you loved anything other than your spells, you'd be late too." She reached back and tidied up her hair, the only cost of her flying spell.

"I do love doing something else, but I need you to do it with." He started to reach for her breast.

She smacked his hand. "Time for that later." Letin looked hurt, but that didn't stop Vulia from continuing. "I had to stop and conduct some business for the Order of the Holy."

"I had Cabal business to get to, and I still made it on time."

"Another defection?" She let her hands drop to her sides, her hair now in place.

"Another termination." He smiled.

"Quietly this time, I hope." She thought back to the first time he had gone on an enforcement mission and how badly it turned out. A whole village had chased him for almost a full day before he got away.

"I used Time Stop and set up a nasty trap. When the spell ran out…" He laughed and used his hands to make the shape of an explosion. "Boom. No more problem."

"You need to be more subtle."

"I was using my new Ethereal spell. I almost have it perfected. I was not only invisible, but I was closer to our master.

Once I was in a safe place inside the traitors' palace, I came out and let the fool have it."

"Could you feel the Master's power?" She rubbed her womb and sorrowed in it being empty.

"I believe I could." Letin sighed. "Even though he wanders lost in the infinite space of the Ethereal plane, I feel like our master wants to stay near us. Well, as close as his boundless prison lets him. So he can watch and bless us until we can finally secure his return."

"If I could bear a vessel for his return, I would have by now." It was her turn to look hurt.

"Let us try." He pawed at her breast again. "Now..."

She knew she couldn't hold him and his addiction off any longer—and besides, even with his poor skills as a lover, it would feel better than the emptiness that was starting to consume her. For ten years they had worked on this plan, and though the physicality between them was new, it was already a bit tiresome. Ten years ago, they'd found the Oil of Etherealness and there, wandering the shadowy, endless plains of the Ethereal plane, the one who would become their master. He would finally return to Holimoren if she could get a seed to grow in her—Letin's seed, any man's seed, she didn't care. As Letin clumsily had his way with her, she started into the same daydream of the Master she'd been having recently. It was the one where, off in the infinite emptiness of the Ethereal, a shadowy outline of a man floated around, the same way he had for hundreds of years. Sensing the thoughts of his favorite pupil, he smiled. She presented him with a vessel, and he floated out of his prison. Emerging onto this plane, he dropped to one knee and proposed to her. She would be his queen.

If only she could be mother to his vessel first.

SIX

Brightside

The dawning of a new morn brings a fresh light,
but does not always bring a better day.
—M'kill the Vicious

Gryphilix had expressed his hope to Dar that with the dawn would come enough sun to burn off the fog. His hope had been dashed. With the sun would have come enough heat to warm up the lizards to get them going—now he had to improvise. Dar watched as he started a fire and laid some heavy knit blankets around it to catch the heat. Once they were hot, Gryphilix placed them on the back of each lizard in turn. He had just rotated the blankets when Yspeida cried, "Alarm!"

Dar pulled out his bow and knocked one of his arrows. He turned to see where Yspeida was pointing: three slate-gray, gruesome-looking monsters were approaching through the woods. Their noses were as long as half-grown carrots, and each arm ended in long, spindly fingers tipped with long, silver claws. Their drooling mouths were filled with small teeth the color of a drab metal and shaped like daggers. There wasn't a single hair on any of their bodies, nor was there much intelligence behind their black eyes. They had smelled the burning wood and the heating wool, it seemed, and figured on an easy meal of mutton or peasants. The group was led by the tallest of the group, and the shortest was trailing behind by about three steps. The middle one was the fattest of the three, and it too was struggling to keep up with the tall one. Dar could see that these were effective killing machines, and if they got onto the coach wagon—or at the lizards—it would be disastrous.

"Rock Trolls!" yelled Dar, and he ran out toward them a little to put some space between him and the coach—he wanted to have a fallback position if needed. Yspeida, hearing that her alarm had been acknowledged, drew both Hack and Slash and went charging toward the trolls. Bounce started collecting the passengers into the coach wagon, and Gryphilix blindly tossed the last of the blankets on the lizards, leaving nothing near the fire for a moment. The newcomer trailed toward the back, and Drij ran into her. Together they hid next to the coach wagon—Drij next to one of the large wheels, and the halfling behind it, under the coach.

"You picked a great time to join our caravan, didn't you, Miss…?"

"Knock. You don't fight, do you?"

"No. Drij is my name."

"Can the three of them take these vile creatures?" Knock looked the monsters over. Even the short one was over twice her height.

"Dar can take one, Yspeida should be able to take one, and Gryphilix probably could take one as well. If not more."

"That's not very inspiring." She contorted her whole face into a frown. "*Can, should,* and *probably* are three friends that don't build my confidence."

They watched as Dar let loose an arrow at medium range—Yspeida was still closing the distance. The trolls lumbered on, doing their version of a trot, which was still slower than a man could run. The arrow Dar fired sailed through the air and hit the lead troll square in the leg. It bounced off. Dar pulled out another and waited, presumably for the distance to shorten, before he tried again.

As he waited, Yspeida had gotten into hand-to-hand range with the lead troll. As she got into her attack position, the lead troll stopped and swung at her. His attack being as slow as he was, Yspeida dodged out of the way and countered with a sweeping motion from one of her swords. The metal blade met the skin of the troll, and a loud ringing noise echoed to the trees beyond. No damage. Yspeida took a small step back and waited to make her next move. As she waited, the other two trolls overtook their comrade, keeping on course at the same speed, headed right at coach wagon.

Dar shot again, this time at the fat troll. His arrow arced through the air and missed its head by a small margin. The troll didn't even bother to move its head—it just kept plodding forward.

Yspeida's foe had finally decided to swing at her again, and this time she ducked under the massive incoming fist and pushed her other sword forward in a thrusting fashion with all of her considerable strength. The blade flexed as it struck the broad chest of the troll, and instead of an echoing ring, a snapping noise radiated away from the battle. Yspeida spun out of the close combat and looked at the damage done to her pride and joy. Drij could see from where he stood beside the wheel of the coach wagon that the sword had been snapped off a third of the way down—her three-foot blade was now a two-foot blade.

"That's not good," Knock remarked.

"How good are you in a battle?" Drij was starting to think about his own battle skills.

"Time to find out." She grinned and stepped out from cover and started toward the trolls.

As Dar's old friend Knock headed toward his position, he pulled back another arrow and again went at the fat troll. This time his aim was true, and the arrow hit the left cheek of the troll's grimacing face. Just like Yspeida's sword, the arrow shivered on impact—splinters flew everywhere. One of those splinters got into the eye of the troll, though, and it stopped to wipe the debris away. When it opened its eyes again, Gryphilix swooped down from the sky and crashed his morning star down on its head. The damage was catastrophic, as the top of its skull collapsed under the pressure and the troll fell to the ground.

Dar paused to watch the fat troll collapse, and then Knock ran past him. Yspeida had moved back, and the troll was still after her. She moved in a slow circle, brandishing Slash at the beast, but not near enough to damage her last blade. Her movement caused the tall troll to turn its back to the fight, and Knock used her leaping and tumbling skills to get into position to attack the weak flank of the monster. Dar watched as she flew into the air, pulling a short sword out of her garments. Like Yspeida's, her sword made a ringing sound, failing to penetrate the stony skin of the troll.

"Edged or piercing weapons are useless!" Yspeida yelled.

Gryphilix had worked his way into the sky again, but once he got to his attacking altitude, Dar could see, the short troll would be at the coach wagon. Knock worked her way back to the coach wagon and appeared to consider her options.

Dar pulled one of his fat-bodied arrows and took aim at the troll. He notched the arrow, pulled back the drawstring, and let it fly. Just after the string was released, a small piece of wood fell away from the back of the arrow; inside the fat body of the shaft, a small spring previously pushed in by the small piece of wood had struck a flint piece across the face of a combustible material. This caused a small fire, and the material packed into the shaft of the arrow started to burn. With a burning flame and a trail of billowing white smoke behind it, the arrow gained supersonic speed. The arrow hit the troll with such force that it entered the skin of the creature the way a normal arrow would enter normal skin. The vessel containing the burning powder ruptured, and the reaction used for propulsion went from controlled to uncontrolled. The powder covered the wound the arrow tip had caused, burning—and then it exploded. Part of the back of the troll cleaved away from the front, detached, while the front burned with the fury of the Hells. The troll fell backward and didn't move as the fire started to consume its body.

Dar looked at the now-dead troll, and his mind raced with wonderment. Splitting a foe in half was new, even for him. Yspeida dove under the legs of the troll she was battling and ran toward Dar, clearly hoping to give him a clean shot. Dar pulled another of his special arrows out of his quiver. Once Yspeida was clear, he let it fly, with the same results. Knock's mouth dropped open, and he thought he heard her chuckling.

When all three trolls were on the ground, Gryphilix came back down, and the group gathered around Dar.

"What is the story behind those arrows?" the winged man asked. "You need to tell me, for they are the most wondrous magical weapons I have ever seen!"

"Actually, they aren't magical."

Yspeida nodded. "Proves craftsmanship is better than magic."

Dar pulled one out and let everyone look at it. "I was given five score of these by a fellow I did some work for. His name is Mrix Trel and he believes in the power of the mind over the power of magic. He calls them propulsive arrows."

Gryphilix looked at the fat shaft of the arrow. "I call them a miracle."

The assessment of the weapon was interrupted by an alarm from Bounce. "There is a fourth troll!!"

Dar looked around to see if there were more trolls they hadn't accounted for. Seeing the troll that Gryphilix had brought down wasn't where it fell, he couldn't help but admire the regenerative powers of the troll—something the burning impact of the arrow would prevent.

The group broke up their semicircle and let Dar work his special arrow again. This time the arrow didn't cause a cleaving, but the effect was no less deadly. As the fire of the unspent fuel burned the troll, it also spread to the ground, and a small brushfire started.

"Fire! Fire!" Gryphilix yelled.

Knowing that the last troll was most likely already dead, Dar pulled out Winter and rushed over to the brushfire. With a quick wave of the blade, which was glowing a frozen electric-blue color, the fire suddenly stopped. A slight coating of frost could be seen on the grass where he had placed the blade, but it quickly gave way to dew. By stopping the expansion of the flames, Dar helped to create a natural fire pit for the troll to safely burn itself out. Dar quickly made the same for the other trolls, and then slowed down to watch the trolls turn to ashes. As the final one burned its last, Dar inspected the remains up close. A strong smell of sulfur and sugar wafted in the gentle breeze. Its skin might have been like stone, but like all trolls, fire ended them as surely as salt ended the largest of slugs.

During this time the rest of the crew and passengers of the coach wagon had gotten on board and prepared to get moving. The blankets had apparently done the job, because the lizards were warm enough to get going. Once Dar was satisfied that the trolls no longer had any ability to again become a threat, he joined the other passengers. Gryphilix waited until Dar was stowing his stuff before he released the food in front of the lizards. Then, with a lurch, off they raced.

The coach wagon moved along, but not at its normal rate. The lizards still weren't up to full temperature, so they were jogging rather than running. Making things worse, the fog was getting thicker as the morning went along. As the wagon continued into the mist, Gryphilix's expression got more and more tense.. He signaled to Bounce to come and take the reins and then proceeded skyward. Dar went up to the driver's seat and peered into the billowing fog.

"Where is Gryphilix headed?"

Bounce left one hand on the stop lever and focused on the path. "He said something about one lizard being warm than the other, and he took off."

Dar frowned. "That means?"

"If one lizard is warmer, it will be faster…"

"And if it's faster, it will veer the wagon off course." Dar looked to the sky, but Gryphilix was nowhere to be seen. "I'll go back and keep watch."

Dar always became more alert while Gryphilix was gone, and this was no exception. He paced the deck and kept his eyes on the world outside as it passed—the fog was hiding the trees and probably danger. He was so focused on the periphery of the haze that he almost stepped on Knock. She was camped out next to Adalia.

"Hey!" the small woman yelped as Dar kicked her leg.

Dar looked down. He quickly hid a look of recognition behind a mask of bewilderment. "What?"

Her voice was louder than one would expect from her size. "I'm sitting here!"

Dar stepped around her, and once his face was oriented so only Knock could see it, his eyes darted over to Adalia. He opened his eyes extra wide for a moment. He rubbed his chin and then gave a quick bow. "I'm very sorry."

"Don't let it happen again." Knock was much better at hiding her emotions than Dar and gave no reaction to his movements.

"I won't." Dar turned to Adalia and bowed toward her. "Adalia."

Her tone was as cold as Winter. "Dar."

"You're looking lovely this morning." He thought a small bow would be too much.

She fought back a smile, and he could feel the chill in the air warming up a little bit. "Thanks."

Dar winced and walked on. He squinted slightly as his eye went to the edge of the fog, again looking for trouble.

Once Dar was a little ways away, Knock turned to Adalia. "Big fellow like that could do a lady harm, you know?"

"He's a good man." Adalia watched him as he paced. "I'm not sure about him, but that much I do know."

"Handsome too, eh?"

"Yes, but…" Adalia turned to face Knock. "That's a mean trick making me talk about him like that. I mean, he's nice enough. He's not like that winged man—or that lackey Bunch, or whatever his name is. There is something about that one I don't trust."

Knock looked at Adalia with a slight smile. "When you get to be my age, you'll know that there is something about all men you don't ever trust."

Dar had just finished a pacing loop and was heading toward the front part of the coach wagon when Gryphilix landed. He was mad, and his face was wet from flying in clouds and dense fog.

"We have a problem," he began. "We are off course, and the fog is thicker than any fog I have ever seen. It's hiding trouble; that much I know. I heard some goblin voices, about a dozen or two, maybe. I flew up and up, but the fog was topped by clouds. I have never seen this before."

Yspeida walked up, as did Drij.

Dar looked at each before speaking to Gryphilix. "So, we have been off course since we left this morning?"

Gryphilix wiped his face, but the grim look under the wetness remained. "Yes. And at our current speed, we are probably a good five to ten miles off course. That's the difference between hitting Brightside and hitting something I don't even want to mention."

"Either the Gelford Cliffs or the middle of the Goblin Forest," Drij offered.

Yspeida chimed in, "This is the work of magic. I can sense it."

Dar lifted one of his eyebrows and looked at Yspeida. "How can you tell?"

"My people can sense powerful magic. This is a high-order spell; I can feel it in my blood."

Drij looked at Dar. "Weather control is both a high-order clerical spell and a high-order magical spell."

"So this is an attempt to get us to drive straight into an ambush?" Gryphilix's face started to turn red as he spoke.

Dar felt somber. He answered flatly, "I believe so."

Gryphilix looked at each one in turn. "Which one of you is the target?"

Dar turned and walked back to his section of the benches. He reached under his chair and grabbed the shield he had gotten earlier from his magical closet and then returned to them. "As long as we are all on this coach wagon, we all are. Whatever foe is behind this, I bet they don't care how many people they hurt as long as they get their mark. Whoever that might be."

The red in Gryphilix face grew brighter. "Great. All of you are bloody targets, and Gryphilix gets to be the driver for your damned adventure. I ought to charge you each extra."

"Calm down, Gryphilix." Dar flipped over his shield and continued, "This is a magic shield." Yspeida took a step back. "*Espiritus mappsu.*"

Inside the shield, a map of Holimoren appeared. All of the major shapes and features were there, and as they watched, a great number of fine details like cities slowly popped up. Suddenly a red dot appeared on the map. It was several miles below a mark labeled *Brightside*, just a little bit dawnward from the Goblin Forest. A small, hatched line was south of the red dot.

Dar pointed at each feature in turn as he explained the situation. "We are here. This hatched line is the cliffs. We need to stop and turn sharply right, so we'll come at the town from the south."

Gryphilix studied the map, his eyes darting over the marked areas. After a moment of thought, he left the conversation in haste and took control of the coach wagon.

Drij continued to study the shield, and then he pointed at some of the lettering. "Why do some of the towns have green lettering and some have black? See, *Holin* is green, but *Brightside* is black. And there are the elven cities…"

"*Mappsu endii.*" Dar picked up the shield and started to carry it back to his bench but then turned back to Drij. "And before you think about using it, it's trained to my voice. You might know the command words, but that won't allow you to work it."

"But I just wanted…"

"Never mind. When you tell your story, Drij, I'll tell mine. How's that?"

Out of the corner of his eye, Dar could see Yspeida watching and no doubt wondering about him. She had to be torn. Because of her culture, she would probably admire his fighting ability, but because he used magic, she would think him a monster. Suddenly the wagon shook violently and jostled everyone around.

They were now heading north.

A short time later, as the coach wagon finally made it out of the fog and entered the clear afternoon sun, Drij walked up to Dar who was sitting at his spot on the bench. Dar was doing his meditations. Drij sat next to him and, as before, started his own. Dar peeked at Drij, whose eyes were already closed.

"I meant no harm." Drij didn't open his eyes while he spoke.

"I know." Dar closed his eyes while he answered. "Sometimes we mean well, but we just don't do well."

"So, what do you know about Brightside?"

"It is a fairly new town, built as a mining camp. Because of a quirk of the landscape, it gets more sun than the surrounding area—the mountains and hills have made a little gap that allows the center of town to get more sun than the shadows of the valleys."

"Is it evil?" Dar was sure he could hear some doubt in Drij's voice.

"I don't know." Dar tried to sound assuring.

"Yes it is." Both men opened their eyes—Knock was standing before them. "And the Holy are to blame for most of its current bent in the direction of self-destruction."

"Dar, this is Knock." Drij's formal tone gave way to an angrier one. "I'm sure you don't know what you're talking about, madam."

Knock was standing while Drij was down in the lotus position, but they were eye to eye. "Seen it with my own eyes,

I have. There was evil before them, but the true believers were able to keep it in check and keep the people directed and happy. Then the Holy came into town and changed it all."

Drij scoffed at the idea. "The Holy didn't make that town evil."

"They did chase away those that kept that town good." She turned her back to him. "That's evil in my book."

"I'm sure that was just something that happened at the same time."

She spun around in the blink of an eye. "There are three things I don't believe in. First is love at first sight, second is luck, and third is coincidence. Things happen for a reason. Either it was the Holy or it was Cabal. And I ain't seen much of those magic-using wretches around here. They tend to be a little hard to miss. Egos the size of the Spire!"

Dar blinked. "Cabal?"

"Oh, so finally you show some respect for the smaller folk around and open your eyes!" She chuckled. "Yeah, the Cabal."

Drij took a deep breath, putting his anger in check. "What is the Cabal?"

"You don't travel much, do you, fancy man?" She took a seat on their bench, which put her just slightly higher than eye level with the men as they sat with their legs crossed on the floor of the coach wagon. "The Cabal is a formerly secret brotherhood that is looking for some ancient power so they can understand all of magic and then use it to take over the world."

"Really?" It seemed as if Drij couldn't have put more sarcasm into the word if he'd tried.

Knock smiled. "That's the funny part about evil. It's not good enough to take over a section or two or even a whole region. Gotta be the whole world. Even half of Holimoren isn't enough for them. I can't ever figure it out. But since I ain't evil, I doubt I ever will."

"And you, Miss Halfling, will stop them?" Drij started to get up, but Dar could tell that the confrontation had made him too tense to immediately unfold.

"Oh no, not me or my folk." She pushed her way off of the bench and stood, again, eye to eye with the struggling Drij. "Only time and the True Gods can stop evil. Mankind can fight it better than the rest, but they seem to be too busy looking for the glimpses of sunshine to want to fight away the clouds. But my folk, we work to stop the little evils, the personal ones that sometimes grow up to be truly evil."

She looked Drij in the eye. "People like those in the Holy end up working with the Cabal by accident or on purpose. When you stray away from doing good and stop believing in the works of the True Gods, you're letting evil win." She raised her chin slightly. "You are evil."

Drij shook his head. "Glad to learn your moral compass is the one we should all follow. I thought all my years in the religious orders would give me some direction, but here it was, just waiting for me in the form of a bitter halfling woman." Drij stood as he finished the last part of his tirade. "Move along and sell your stories of morality to somebody who might listen, short one."

Knock walked off in disgust. "You'll see, Drij the Wanted."

Dar just closed his eyes and went back to his meditations. "How did she know who I am?"

Dar didn't move a muscle. "How do any of us know who we are?"

Dar could hear Drij make a grumbling sound. "So why do I feel suddenly very hunted?"

Far ahead of the coach wagon, a thin man in long black robes sat sipping tea in the tavern of the inn he was staying at. Across the street, in view of his vantage point near the window, was the Brightside stop of the Gryphilix wagon line. He could tell by the lengthening shadows outside that the coach was late. He rotated his head around in a small circle and eased the tension out of his neck. Not the tallest of men, just short of six feet by an inch or two, he wasn't a fighter, and he wasn't much of a lover. But he could use magic like few ever could, and the longer the coach wagon was late, the more prominent the smirk on his face became. Thin, even for a mage, he found little amusement in food. He was in fine health, but wouldn't win any fisticuffs. Well, until he started using his spells. He took another sip of the lemon tea. It helped his voice, and he had been doing lots of talking. All of it recruiting.

When he finished his second cup, the coach wagon was over two hours late, an excellent sign. He was just about to order another pot of the voice-soothing fluid when the lizards came into view. The rest of the coach wagon stopped just out of sight, but that could be fixed quickly. He placed a handful of coins on the table—just enough to pay the bill, no tip—and walked out. Once outside he studied the semi-ordered mess that was the unloading of the coach wagon. A quick survey showed no damage to the wagon. He counted heads. There was one more than there was supposed to be. Not only had the goblin ambush failed, they had picked up another fool.

He could hear the winged man that ran the operation start talking to the pathetic rabble that was just getting ready to leave, going through the exiting procedures.

"We will be staying in Brightside for the night and leaving first thing in the morning. You're welcome to sleep onboard the coach wagon or at any of the town's fine accommodations. I will use the whistle as usual, but I will give you three warnings. After that, I will leave you here. Boarding for new passengers can begin right away."

The tall man had heard enough. He walked back into the inn and back up to his room. He had to think, and thinking around the unwashed masses made him want to vomit. With a small bottle of a clear liquid and his book of spells, he lay in his bed and stayed up all night thinking. He couldn't ask for help—this was his operation, and he had allowed it to fall apart.

By the time dawn arrived, the liquid was gone, his book was closed, and he was sleeping. When the first whistle blew, he started to stir, slightly hungover from his battle with the bottle. By the time the second whistle blew, he knew his course of action and was heading out of the inn. Gryphilix was just counting heads and getting the whistle ready when he walked up to him.

"My good man, I'd like a place on your transport."

"Sure. How far you going?"

"A couple of days."

"Five gold."

"Here you go." The tall man placed the amount in silver into his hands. Gryphilix looked down at the fifty coins and rolled his eyes.

"Sit anywhere."

"Don't you want my name? Perhaps for a passenger manifest—or to put in your journal?"

"Don't particularly care, sir. Your name is your problem."

He stepped away from Gryphilix and boarded at the back. The youth who met him there did not seem to recognize him, though the tall man knew who Bounce was at once. Bounce offered his hand to help him up. As their eyes met, the tall man said, "My name is Letin. You know my sister."

SEVEN

Passion Play

Two things motivate all people: fear and love.
—King Albacas the Fourth

The lizards sped off toward their next stop, and Letin took his position in the Box. He could smell her here, even though it had been a couple of days since she'd left. (He could always smell her—it was like an opiate; it made him dreamy, always broke his concentration.) In his profession you needed to have a good sense of smell and taste to stay one step ahead of the next dose of poison. The lackey had been helpful, and this room would more than serve his needs. He would assess the situation and make off with the vessel. That would show Vulia that he was capable of doing the legwork too. A knock at the door brought him back into the present.

"Yes?" he growled at the door.

"It's the porter, Bounce."

"Come in."

Letin could tell by the look on his face that this Bounce person was not impressed by the wizard's physical stature. His mind raced for moment, darting around this odd encounter. How much had Vulia talked about him to this thug? She hadn't said that the cutpurse would come to see him in the box. Did this mean Bounce realized there had been a change in plans?

"Why are you here?" Bounce was keeping his voice low.

Letin took in a deep breath and let it out while he spoke. "Why was the coach wagon late?"

"We got lost in the fog and had to come at the city from below. We had to ford a river, and it took awhile to get the lizards warm again."

"The fog?" He had cast that spell to keep the movement of the goblins away from prying eyes. "No matter. Vulia has put me in charge now. I'll take care of things directly."

"As you wish." Bounce tipped his head forward and slowly brought it back up.

Letin was sure he saw the smallest of knowing grins at the mention of his sister. "Who is onboard that is a risk to me in taking the vessel?"

"There is a ranger with magic spells and lots of magic weapons, a barbarian female, and a halfling who has great agility and tumbling skills. She must be a powerful thief or fighter thief."

"Any others?" Letin narrowed his eyes as he absorbed the new information.

"The merchant used to be a powerful cleric but has joined the Holy and has lost his spells."

Letin smiled. The ruse of the Holy claimed another. "How is the winged man?"

"You can operate freely when he goes to scout ahead." Bounce smiled. "But you'll need to work quickly."

"Excellent." Letin smirked. He preferred to work quickly.

"Vulia didn't say that you were going to join the coach wagon."

"Plans change." Letin clenched his jaw and fist. "When does the winged one leave for his next flight?"

"In about an hour. I do the driving during that time, so I will knock on the door as I go past to take control."

"Good." Letin wondered how much Vulia had shared of their plan. Or of herself. "Now get out."

Dar sat on the floorboards with his legs in the lotus position again. Drij was alongside him again, although his legs were just crossed. Dar was deep in meditation, the forces of magic flowing through him. He could feel his own magic, along with the chaos from those around him that made his magic hard to control. But then he felt another force on the magic. He looked at Drij. The ebbs and flow around him were steadying. Dar smiled as he closed his eyes again. Drij must have been close to being able to cast spells again, at least the minor magicks that acknowledging the True Gods would bring. He would have to talk to Drij about it. He had just about settled back into his meditative trance when a voice rang out and ruined his moment of understanding.

"Hey!" It was Knock. Bounce had accidentally kicked her in the leg as she lay on the floorboards.

"Sorry." Bounce had a sheepish look showing he was honestly sorry he had run into her. He continued up to the driving chair, slowing for just second near the entrance to the Box. Dar thought he saw Bounce rap the door to the Box softly, but he had just enough doubt to keep him away from action. Bounce was securely in the driving chair for when the new passenger came out of the Box. The newcomer walked back and stopped near the middle of the coach wagon. Dar stood while he assessed the situation. The newcomer sat near the middle, with Yspeida, Adalia, and Knock, but Dar and Drij were closer to the back of the seating area. He decided to close the distance. Just in case.

Dar walked down the side row of the coach wagon and stopped for a second when he reached Adalia. She was looking a little down in the mouth.

"Is everything all right?" he asked.

"Yes." She paused. "No. I guess."

Dar kneeled next to her but turned a little so his back wasn't to the newcomer. "Tell me about it."

"I met Trypia a year ago today."

The mention of her former lover's name caused both of them to wince a little in pain.

"I'm sorry," was all that Dar could figure out to say.

"Me too." She rubbed May's box.

"Don't let the memory of that monster of a man hurt you any further," offered Yspeida. She came over, but as she did, she seemed to get nervous and stopped short. She pulled out Slash and Hack (though the second sword wasn't really functional as a weapon anymore). "Something isn't right."

Dar looked at her wounded weapon. "I know you hate magic, but I can fix that sword."

"That's just it." She leaned into him and whispered, "There is powerful magic nearby."

Dar looked at the newcomer, who averted his eyes from the conversation. "All the more reason for me to fix that for you. How about it?"

She paused, her eyes narrowing. Dar could see her whole body tense up. "Only because you have fought alongside me in battle." She handed him the fragment from the blade along with the rest of the weapon.

"Once the spell is over, it won't be magical anymore," he assured her. "It will just be your sword. The magic will only last a moment." He put the two parts together and mumbled the magic words of the Mending spell. The sword began to glow like the sun, and everyone else had to avert their eyes. When the blazing glow subsided, the sword was in one piece again. He handed it back to Yspeida.

"It is whole again." She danced her way through her practice maneuvers. It had regained its perfect balance. She halted her practice and closed her eyes, as if feeling the rushing flow of the nearby magic. "I sense only the magic of the power at hand." She shifted her stance to face Dar. She looked him in the eye. "Maybe magic isn't pure evil."

"Magic is a tool," Dar said. "It is the user who makes it good or evil."

The newcomer stood and walked back toward the front. He stood facing the Box for a moment. Dar couldn't see what he was doing, but it all seemed safe enough. He looked at Bounce, reigns in hand. Even from the steps you could see the driver.

Bounce looked ahead on the road. This job had gotten out of hand, and this Letin guy was sure to be trouble.

"I'm altering the plan further." The voice spoke in Bounce's right ear. He went to turn to see where it was coming from, but before he could, it said, "Don't move. It is Letin. I'm using a magic spell to talk to you. Don't act like you can hear anything."

Bounce turned his eyes in his head as far to the right as he could, but he couldn't see anyone. He slowly raised and lowered his head, like he was stretching.

"Here is what you need to know about the new plan. This wagon is too small for me to survive any armed combat. I need you to help even the odds. When I tell you the command word 'now,' you will stab the ranger in the back. Make sure it ends him." There was a pause. "Tug the reins if you understand."

It was Bounce's turn to pause. Then he gave the leather straps that controlled the lizards a pull.

"Also, there will be another passenger on board shortly. Do nothing about it. Your only concern is my command word."

Bounce nodded as if he had been jostled by the road. He heard the door to the Box open and shut, and he celebrated with a deep breath followed by a sharp exhale.

He couldn't believe the way this was getting worse and worse. First he was just to keep an eye out for things and to signal when the conditions were right. Then he was to help set them up for an ambush. Now it was about murder. Even sleeping with that blond woman, as much fun as that had been, wasn't making up for this. He was a petty thief, not a criminal. He wondered what these two would be asking him to do next. Whatever it was, he wouldn't touch the dead girl.

Even by his limited code of honor, the dead were something you didn't touch.

He hoped Gryphilix wouldn't return for a while. He needed to think about his next step, and he had to prepare a good story for why there was going to be another person onboard.

Gryphilix had returned and left again by the time the door to the Box opened once more. The group was loafing around the coach wagon, and Dar had noticed that Bounce kept looking over his shoulder, seemingly looking for something that hadn't happened yet. Now, perhaps, the event he'd been anticipating had arrived: the person who'd stepped out of the Box was a tall blond man—not thin and spindly like the newcomer, this man was muscular, and his skin was bronze. But his body didn't suggest a tan earned by hard work—it seemed more like a costume choice of the rich and vain.

"Hello, Adalia."

Adalia's head shot up quicker than Dar had seen her move. She mumbled something that Dar couldn't understand. Then she started to stand, but it seemed as if her legs wouldn't work. She started to speak again, but still no words came out.

Yspeida had no such troubles. "Back off, you foul man!" She rushed over to put herself between the newcomer and Adalia, stopping his progress. It appeared that Adalia was using the delay to compose herself.

Dar was at the rear end of the coach wagon when the commotion started but was immediately on the scene. Adalia had finally found her legs and was standing—getting ready for a battle, it would appear.

"I have come back to you to honor my marriage proposal." The muscular man, who was obviously Trypia, looked at Adalia with puppy-dog eyes. "I still need you."

He moved forward slightly, but Yspeida blocked his way. Dar watched as Trypia's eyes went down to assess her cleavage and lingered long enough for everyone to notice.

"You must let me talk to her!" Trypia pleaded.

Yspeida appeared not to hear the request. He responded by pushing her. Dar could tell by the way he clumsily pressed up against the she-warrior that he had no formal combat training. Trypia was doing it all wrong. His thrust was working toward her mass and positioning instead of trying to dislodge her. Even a squire knew that when grappling, balance was the key. He was off his center; she was being pushed into hers. Again he pushed hard, but she moved little.

Yspeida looked Trypia in the eye. "You may move forward when she says you can. And if she says to kill you…" She pushed back on him, and he yielded, thrown off balance. "You'll be dead before you hit the ground."

"That isn't necessary." Adalia moved forward, and the fire in her eyes showed she was prepared to fight for herself. It was clear that she had summoned all of her strength to let him have it. "Why did you—?"

Trypia jumped in. "Why did I leave? Why did I not return? Why did I do what I did?" He broke out the puppy-dog eyes again. "I have no defense. I was confused. I was scared. Then I just didn't know what to do. So I ran—"

"Into the arms of a whore?" Adalia laced her words with enough poison to kill a dragon.

"An old friend..." Trypia stepped back, and Yspeida moved with him, giving Adalia some freedom to move. "But then I started to wander around, and I kept thinking of you."

"Thinking of me so much that you didn't write, didn't send a message, and didn't do anything for me during my pregnancy?" Her voice built with every item on her list.

"I said I was scared." Dar noticed Trypia was looking around like he was waiting for something to happen.

"Why should I even talk to you, let alone consider taking you back?" She pressed the advantage.

He looked at her for a second. He looked down and then back at Adalia.

"Because I still..." Dar could tell he was pausing for effect only. "Love you."

Adalia gasped and put her hand to her mouth.

Yspeida turned and gave Trypia a look that could kill. She was clearly still contemplating doing the deed when a cry from Drij came out of the blue. He was away from the discussion, still back at his normal bench spot where it seemed like he hadn't moved from his meditation position.

"Look out!! Somebody is taking the casket!"

The box holding May was floating in midair some distance behind the group. Adalia turned and, seeing the casket that held her baby, fainted dead away. Yspeida's eyes showed the decision she faced—to catch Adalia or try to stop the theft in progress. She reacted with catlike quickness and kicked out just a little behind and beyond the box. It connected with something solid, and the casket and invisible assailant parted ways. In one quick motion, she followed up her kick with a powerful lunge toward the free-falling casket. Diving with grace and fluidity, Yspeida completed the maneuver by grabbing the casket, rolling out, and quickly returning to her feet. Securing her grip on the wood, she made a roundhouse kick, and again she seemed to connect with her target. This time it sounded like the invisible person flew out of the coach wagon altogether.

Dar gently pulled up Adalia from the floor of the coach, brushing the hair out of her face. He watched as Yspeida closed her eyes for a moment, as if she was sensing the area for something. She did not seem to find what she was looking for, because she slowly turned to see how Adalia had fared. Trypia, Dar noticed, was making his way back to the room at the front of the coach wagon.

"Stop, Trypia!" Dar called out. Just then, a blade flew through the air at the fleeing Trypia; Knock had pulled a dagger from up her sleeve. It missed a little to the left, allowing the target to make it to the safety of the Box.

Drij had gotten up when Adalia had fallen, and Dar signaled him immediately.

"Take her—I need to get Trypia. Something is going on here."

"I've got her. Go." Drij lowered himself to the floor and cradled her head in his hands, trying to keep her steady despite the continual rocking of the speeding coach. "*Go!*"

Dar ran for the door. Knock was already there, banging on the door with her small shoulder. Dar leveled his shoulder at the door and gave it a good shove, with no results. He tried again, but the heavy wooden door was locked from the inside.

"Step back, Knock. I'm going to try a spell."

Knock took a step back, and by the time her second step touched the decking of the coach wagon, the spell with which she shared a name was already complete. They could hear the spell magic working, moving the heavy iron fitting inside the door. Dar leveled his shoulder again and pushed the door open.

The room was empty.

When Dar and Knock got back to the scene of the attempted crime, they found Adalia up and about, clutching her baby's casket to her chest once again.

"Who would do such a thing?" she said, trying to control her sobbing. But the fear combined with the sorrow, it seemed, only made her start to hyperventilate. Dar motioned to her to sit down.

"It's okay. They are gone."

"Trypia is gone?" She looked into his eyes. Hers were bloodshot from crying, and Dar could see dark circles forming under them.

"So is the newcomer."

"His name is Letin." Bounce had come down from the driver's seat. Dar looked and saw Gryphilix back at the controls. Bounce went on to say, "He is some sort of magic user."

Adalia sat down, almost on top of Drij. He moved out of the way but started to gently message her back. Dar could tell she was all tension, and he couldn't blame her. Looking at Drij—there was something about him. An air of fatherly concern, yes, but he kept looking at his hands. Like there was something on them that he couldn't trust wasn't really there. Drij's chest began to move rapidly in and out. He was blinking a lot—was he lost in a memory?

"If you're okay," Drij blurted out to Adalia, "I need to get back to my meditations."

She nodded, and he withdrew back to his meditation area. As he started his breathing exercises, Dar could see that a calm came over him, washing away the dire memories that haunted him.

Adalia had a while to go before she would be that calm.

So would Dar.

Dar wondered if Yspeida ever got that calm.

And Knock was already sleeping.

When the coach wagon stopped for the night, it was in a clearing in an evergreen forest. The bonfire was started just like on the other nights, but Adalia didn't get out of the coach wagon. Yspeida stood guard over her, and Knock kept an eye on the whole thing from next to the bonfire.

As the fire was being built by Bounce, Dar had walked off deep into the forest and found a small clearing. He doubled back a couple of times to make sure he wasn't being followed, and then, assured that he was alone, pulled out the magic door and placed it on the ground. He uttered the magic words and stepped inside again.

The extra-dimensional space was eight feet by six feet and was ten feet high, highly tailored for his use. Against the wall to one side sat another shield, an extra sword, and several sacks full of gold, silver, and platinum coins, a bag full of gems, and a small chest. A suit of splint-mail armor hung from the opposite wall, along with an oversized quiver full of the fat-bodied arrows. Next to the hanging items was a series of shelves. A large book of spells—Dar's master book—lay open on one of the shelves. Along the back was a series of nooks that held a variety of potions, scrolls and rods, staves and wands. Other small magic items were stashed in the little cubbyholes. Even the ceiling held items: a large pack of iron rations hung from leather straps.

The air in the room was fresh, and a soft breeze greeted his senses as he stepped in. He walked over to the small chest and opened it. Inside were two bands of gold—one was shiny and looked brand new, while the other was black and pitted. Behind them was a hand mirror. The mirror's frame and handle were made of the finest silver, and not a spot of tarnish could be seen. The surface of the glass was also of perfect smoothness and cleanliness, even the spot where the black, sooty ring lay. He picked up the two rings and the mirror and stuck them in his knapsack. He closed the chest and went over to the cubbyholes, where he picked out a small pewter cup and put it into the bag as well. He looked around for a moment, and then he walked out.

And there was Drij.

"It's not every day you see a door in the middle of a forest." Drij smiled. "Especially one without anything behind it. A door to nowhere, it seems."

Dar sighed. He was glad he had put everything away before coming out. "How did you find me?"

"I was at the camp when I saw a shape nearby. I ran after it and figured out it was a big pig—a boar, really. He looked like he knew the area, so I used an incantation and talked to him about finding food. He told me about some truffles and was showing me the way. I wasn't too interested in the slime pool he wanted to talk about."

"You have access to your spells again?"

A shrug and a meek smile showed Dar this was still a work in progress. "At least a couple of the basics, it seems."

"That's great." Dar smiled but then turned sour again. "But I'm still mad at you."

Drij did not appear to register this, as he was looking behind Dar. "What is it?" Drij asked.

"Closet of Xio."

"Xio?" Drij looked back at Dar. "You mean, *the* Xio?"

Dar turned and uttered the magic phrase softly. The door shrunk until it fit into the palm of his hand. He picked it up. "Yes. The Xio."

"Impressive." Drij just stood there as Dar started walking back to the campsite. "Emperor Xio, magic user and traveler extraordinary. Founder of Magrican—a real ladies' man and general nice guy."

"One of the founders," Dar called back, deadpan.

"Where did you get it?" Drij called in turn.

"I don't have to answer that." Dar kept walking.

Drij raced to catch up. "You understand that I need to know. That thing must be over three hundred years old. That's not something you'd find in a roadside trinket shop. There has to be a story attached. Did you slay the dragon that kept it under lock and key?"

"Actually, yes." Dar made a beeline to the wagon.

"Really?" Drij's eyes opened wider.

"No."

Drij stopped, but Dar kept going. "I really must know," Drij said.

Now it was Dar's turn to stop. "Fine. I'll trade you stories. I'll tell you how I got the closet if you tell me what your crime is."

Drij stopped too, shifting on his feet as if he had been punched. "That is one hell of a trade, my friend."

"We both have our secrets, and if you want me to share, you need to share too."

"Nobody else will find out?" Drij narrowed his eyes.

"Same for you." Dar matched Drij's expression.

"And you'll honor your word to get me to Redemption?"

Dar nodded.

"Your word, please."

"You have my word of honor, that I, Dar Aurlyss, will get you to Redemption no matter your crime."

Drij nodded. "Fine. I agree to the swap. You go first."

"Your word of honor that you'll tell me your story?"

"You have my word of honor, that I, Drij Bahara, will honor my pledge."

Dar watched Drij during his tale, waiting for a reaction. "It was given to me by Xio's son Xing. I did some work for Xing, and he gave me the closet as thanks for the effort. It actually involved slaying a Dark Naga, not a dragon. I killed a dragon for a tinkerer named Mrix Trel. That was how I got the propulsive arrows, the fat-bodied ones. But that is more than we agreed to disclose."

"But Xio and his line have lived in Venge Kleptocracy for over a hundred years. How did you get that far into the Evil lands?"

Dar lifted an eyebrow. "I told my tale and will answer no more."

Drij dropped his head. He knew it was his turn, but clearly, it was hard.

"You must tell me—you promised." Dar wouldn't have normally pressed him, but a deal was a deal.

"I know. But you mustn't look at me. Let us start walking toward the camp, with you in front, so I can't see your face."

"Fine."

They started walking, and after about five paces, Drij finally spoke. "I killed four people." He sounded like he was forcing the words from his mouth.

"I've killed more than that, but I'm not proud of it." Dar tried to make his tone reassuring, but he wasn't sure if it worked.

"These weren't just any people. I killed my son, my two daughters, and my wife." Drij took in a deep breath. "I butchered them, each in turn, and my hands are still covered in their blood."

Dar wrinkled his brow and grimaced slightly. He kept walking, glad Drij was behind him.

"I did it for reasons I'm not fully certain I understand." Dar could hear Drij's breathing change. It sounded like he was taking short, sharp breaths, a sure sign of tears.

"I need to get to Redemption so I can kill myself and join my family. I deserve death, not them."

From then they walked in silence, with only the sounds of Drij's trying to clear his tear-congested nose to mark the passing of time.

Dar didn't dare say a word. He didn't know what to say.

When they got back to the campsite, things were just as they had left them. Yspeida was still at the ready, Knock was watching Adalia from a distance, and the bonfire still roared. What was new was the look on Bounce's face. He seemed to be very mad—or at least very frustrated. But he was working near the coach wagon, and Dar couldn't be bothered to figure out what was going on.

Dar stepped into the light of the bonfire and made an announcement to account for the time they'd been gone. "Drij and I found a pig out in the woods. Drij used a spell, and we talked to the pig about slime pools, but we didn't find the truffles he promised."

It was obvious that Drij appreciated the effort Dar was putting on, because he chimed in, "I figured the group wouldn't like the slime pool, so we just passed."

"Why didn't you kill the pig?" Gryphilix spouted off from just outside the bonfire's circle of illumination. "The lizards can always use more supper."

"It's bad karma to eat things that you've just had a conversation with," Dar said. It was a matter of truth.

"That's why I don't talk to my food." Gryphilix had barely finished his sentence when he started to laugh.

Dar smiled, but Drij had to fake his. Knock seemed to notice this, because she looked over at Dar. Dar felt the weight of her glance, and when their eyes met, he nodded softly. Knock's eyes darted away to Adalia. She was sleeping now, and Yspeida stood guard. Dar watched as Knock stood up and walked over to Yspeida.

"My turn on guard." She smacked Yspeida on her backside. "You've been a great friend and a great warrior, but now you must rest, my sister. I will stand guard over her and lay down my own life, if necessary, to protect hers. I will honor your effort by guarding her the way you would."

Dar could tell by the look on her face that Yspeida wanted to keep the watch, but he knew from his own experience that her body would betray her if she did the overnight shift. The stress of combat followed by the boredom of standing watch made for a powerful sleeping aid. Dar was happy when she nodded to the short woman and then left for her bedroll on the deck of the coach wagon.

Dar was awoken by Knock's foot. It was a gentle push, not like other times he could think of. He blinked the sleep from his eyes and looked around. The moon was just before the highest point in its rise. It appeared everyone was finally asleep. Even Gryphilix had nodded off.

"What did you do to Gryphilix?" Dar whispered, not sure how asleep everyone was.

"It took a small pinch of sleeping powder from my bag of tricks." Knock laughed, not lowering her voice at all. "Everything is ready." She pulled out a small bronze compass and pointed it one direction then another. Satisfied with its readings, she motioned to Dar.

"Time to go," was all she said.

EIGHT

Two Minutes to Midnight

Only a handful of happenings go on during the
dark of midnight, and none of them are things
you can tell your children.
—Elader the Old

Letin stood while Trypia tried to find a comfortable spot on
the lumpy bed. They were in a tower in the town of Hol
Amroth—thankfully, the thick stone walls kept the room well
insulated from the sounds of the town and the cold of the
winds that this area was famous for. Letin rubbed his stomach,
noting that his arm now bore a large bruise in the shape of a
foot. Trypia kept closing his eyes, but every time his breathing
got too regular, Letin hit his foot or shook the bed.

"You know, you don't have to keep me awake," Trypia
said, fighting a yawn.

"You need to be awake when she gets here," Letin growled
at him.

"Trust me, I'm always ready to meet a lady."

"Back off, lover boy." He turned and looked Trypia in the eye. "You're only here because you triggered my ring of recall. Once I finish this business here, I'll send you back home until I need you again."

"No problem." Trypia laughed.

Vulia entered the room and quickly shut the door. She was expecting Letin, but not his handsome friend. "Who is this?"

"Trypia. Father of the vessel."

Trypia came to his feet, rushed over to Vulia, and gently kissed her outstretched hand. "Enchanted to meet you, Miss…"

"Vulia." She batted her eyes. "The pleasure will be all mine."

"I hope so." Trypia winked at her.

"You two make me sick." Letin did his best to kill the mood. "Can we talk about our problem for a moment?"

"First explain how this Trypia came to be involved in our problem." Vulia pulled a comb out of the dresser and started to brush her hair. She knew it drove Letin crazy, but she clearly wasn't preening for him.

Letin tried to ignore her efforts. "When she mentioned his name, I went to their town, found him, and bought his help. I only used Trypia as a distraction."

"But it didn't work." Trypia smoothed back his own hair. "And he got kicked by some barbarian woman."

"Isn't she from the same tribe that you raided during our first search for a vessel?" Vulia asked.

Letin scowled. "She is. But more importantly, I think they know that the vessel is what we are after."

Vulia turned and stopped combing. She stared at Letin with evil intent and paused for a moment, apparently deciding on a course of action. "Failure seems to be the only thing you're good at, Letin." She resumed her brushing. "Leave the room now. I wish to interrogate Trypia about the mother of the vessel."

"But I can help," Letin begged.

"No, you can't." She smiled, knowing it would hurt him.

He pleaded with his eyes. Hers were solid ice, and his heart started to wither.

"There is a room next door. Wait there until the morning."

"Yes, sister."

Letin walked over to the door and made his way to the adjoining room. He sat next to the window and stared at the moon as it crossed its zenith for the evening. The wind blew, but he liked the cold. Then he heard them talking—the window to the room next door was open. He could hear the sounds, but he couldn't make out any words. Then there came a long, heavy pause and occasional noises of happenings that blurred into the noise of the wind. The silence was then broken by the screams of her passion and finally the grunts of his satisfaction.

After that Letin could only hear the sound of his heart breaking and the fire of anger in it burning brighter than ever.

Dar shook Adalia softly, and she started to stir. She opened her mouth to scream, apparently alarmed to find a man standing over her, but before anything could come out, Dar had placed his hand gently on top.

"Shhhh." He leaned in close. "We need to talk, and we need to protect May."

Adalia relaxed a little as she recognized Dar. She nodded to indicate that she wouldn't scream, and he released his hand.

She sat up, and he moved back to give her some room. That's when she noticed Knock.

"Why is she here?" She pointed at the small woman.

"Knock is an associate of mine," Dar told her, "and she has come aboard to help me figure out what is going on. You can trust her with your life, as I have on many an occasion. She is not what she seems, so do not underestimate her abilities."

Adalia looked at Knock with new eyes. She nodded her agreement.

"What I am going to tell you tonight, you tell no one," Dar went on. "I can help you and May get safely to Redemption, but you must do what I say, and you must swear on your life not to mention any of the plan to anyone."

Adalia looked him in the eye so he could see the truth in her eyes. "If it is for May, I'd walk to the Hells barefoot and naked."

"Good." He pulled the mirror and the two rings out of his bag. "This is a set of magic items called the Evidence of Faithfulness. It consists of the two Rings of Promise and its partner mirror. The mirror is aptly enough called the Mirror of Proof. Without going into all the details, it allows for the person holding the mirror to see where each of the rings currently resides. I would like you to wear one of the rings, and I have a plan for the other."

He held out the shiny ring, and Adalia took it. She went to place it on her right hand, but it was about three sizes too big. He nodded, and she put it on anyway. As it touched her finger for the first time, the size started to adjust, and by the time it was in position, it was the perfect size for her.

"The other ring is part of the plan to figure out who is after you and May."

She looked at him with trepidation. It was clear she didn't understand.

"I have a place where we can put May where nobody can get to her. Once she is in the safety of this protected place, we will put a small weight and the other Ring of Proof into the casket. Anybody who takes the box will take the ring, and we'll be able to see where they are and who they are with. Then we can counter them."

"You can't take my May."

"She'll be right here with us, just out of sight." Dar gave her a hopeful smile.

"I don't understand." Adalia looked to Knock then to Dar. "You'll make May invisible?"

"I have an extra-dimensional storage space. Consider it a portable closet. I can put things into it, and they stay there, ageless, until I come back for them. I keep all my valuables there, like this mirror and ring set."

"And May will be safe there?" Adalia lowered her chin and squinted one eye slightly.

"Safer than here." Dar moved in close and touched her back. She jerked her shoulder away as she considered his comments.

"And I could see her every night?" She turned her head slightly and squinted at Dar.

"The access to her will be with me, and I can take you to her once we step away from the main group." Dar tried the hopeful smile again.

"And that person you're traveling with won't know?"

Knock nodded as Dar answered. "Only you, Knock, and I will know."

"When will you need to know if I will let you have May?"

Dar looked at Knock, who answered the question. "Maybe ten minutes. Tops. Gryphilix won't stay out for long. If I keep him out sleeping too long, he'll go into hibernation early and we'll be walking to Redemption."

Dar reinforced her answer. "Sooner would work better than later, Adalia."

She nodded and picked up May in her casket. She walked off of the coach wagon and looked to the stars. There were a million points of lights staring back at her, and she seemed to be hoping a god or goddess would come down and help her decide. Dar watched as a streak of light crossed the sky, bright enough to see, but only lasting for a brief moment. Adalia closed her eyes, took a deep breath, and turned around. She started walking back to the coach wagon, but Dar met her halfway.

She presented him the casket. "Let's do it."

Dar worked fast to make the switch happen. After opening the closet, he went to the back and picked out one of the finest chests. He dumped its cargo of potions on the floor, and handed it to Knock to finish preparing it for May. He then used a Create Normal Object spell to create a clay doll of May with exquisite detail.

"I want to put May's dress on the doll." Dar went over to the women, who were cleaning out the dirt from the bottom of the chest outside the closet.

"No." Adalia folded her arms. "That is her dress. She keeps it."

"But it will make it more..."

Knock cut him off with a wave of her hand. "You heard her. No."

Dar nodded, knowing better than to cross Knock once she made up her mind.

"Thank you, Knock, for your support." The endearing look Adalia gave Knock showed Dar that a real friendship was blossoming. Dar set down the clay doll by the women and retreated into the closet.

In the back of the closet, where the whispers of the chatting ladies wouldn't distract him, Dar kept himself busy by moving the dumped potions into other storage places. By the time he had them all squared away, he realized Adalia was standing next to him. She presented him with the chest with May in it. Taking it with a solemn bow of his head, he gently placed it on the shelf and then the trio exited in silence.

Adalia spoke the only words uttered during their return to camp. "I hope this works. I miss her already."

With the dawn came a light haze. It was hard to tell if it was smoke or just fog, but it made the campsite feel cold. Dar had woken up well rested. It was the first time since they'd left Holin that he felt like he was finally in command, ahead of the day's events instead of behind them. He had traveled enough to know it was just an illusion, but the ego did enjoy the moment when it came.

Adalia was still sleeping on board the coach wagon when Gryphilix decided to get the group back on the way to Redemption. The whole group seemed to be more reserved than normal. The pace of life on board the coach wagon seemed to be slower. Dar finished his meditations and exercises and just stared out into the distance, watching the trees and hills go by as the coach wagon continued its journey to far-off lands.

Drij also did some meditations and stretching—Dar noticed that he was wearing a belt now, as his pants had gotten looser over the course of the journey on the coach wagon. Yspeida did some stretching as well, curiously without her weapons. Dar told himself to ask her about that later. Knock just kept looking around at the various members of the ragged band, a small smirk occasionally appearing in the corner of her lips. Bounce fidgeted awkwardly at the back of the coach wagon, like he couldn't wait to get off. Dar knew the feeling.

Finally, when the sun had climbed almost halfway to its high point in the sky, Adalia woke up. She was slow moving at first, as if she'd forgotten all of the troubles of the last several months. But Dar could see them returning to her mind as she looked around and recognized all of the people she was traveling with. She reached out with her hand and gently touched the box beside her—it was clear that she knew it was empty but wanted it to be full. It was written on her face: she longed to feel her baby, but knew she couldn't. Dar knew that carrying the fake baby realistically would be the hardest part of the plan. He hoped she would get used to it quickly; otherwise, they were at risk of tipping off the forces marshaled against them. Dar had faith Adalia wouldn't let them down.

Adalia practiced taking the casket for a walk around the coach wagon. As she finished her lap, Dar walked up.

"How are you doing this morning?"

"I slept well."

"As I." He looked her in the eye for a long moment in silence and then at the casket. "How is May?"

"She is as heavy as my heart is, but we are both fine after yesterday's commotion." She smiled lightly, clearly not wanting to give too much away in case somebody was watching.

"I hope today will be quiet."

"As do I." It was clear that she meant it.

Dar nodded and continued to stroll around the coach wagon. He walked past the area where Bounce normally spent his time when he was off duty but didn't find him. Dar casually looked around for him, as did Adalia, but he was nowhere to be seen. Dar walked on, lingering next to Knock for a moment, otherwise keeping his normal pace.

In the Box, out of sight of the world, Bounce took out a small vial of black liquid and placed it on the table in the corner of the room. He took out his dagger and unscrewed the bottom half of the handle. Taking the vial in hand, Bounce opened it up and dumped the fluid into the small opening in the handle. His being extra careful to not get any on him took extra time, and even with that extra effort, he still spilled some on the floor. The liquid ate at the floorboards and turned it black. Bounce screwed the handle together, making the dagger whole again. He scooped up a small pillow off the bed and rubbed it on the stain on the floor. The liquid was now gone, but the pillow had started to turn black wherever the liquid touched it. Bounce opened the door and peeked around the corner, seeing if anyone was watching. Finding no one, he walked out and closed the door behind him. Bounce moved over to the edge of the coach wagon and threw the pillow overboard.

He looked around for Dar, hoping to find the courage he would need to use the weapon.

"Bounce?"

Bounce turned. It was Gryphilix.

"I need you to take control for a while—I need to go flying."

"But we already know the route for today."

His boss was scowling, his face colored with frustration. "I know, but I just can't clear my head. Flying is the only thing I can do that keeps the fog in my head from coming back. I still can't believe that I feel asleep like that. It is still a couple of days before my rest. It is just completely unlike me to have that happen."

"Yeah, okay then." Bounce hoped the courage would come to him while he drove the coach wagon. "I'll drive."

"The last time this happened to me, it was a sleep spell, if my memory serves. My people have always been weak against the spells of sleeping." He sighed, his wings rising and falling like his chest. "I used to have a ward against it, but it was stolen a while back. Just after you joined, I believe. Hol Amroth is a horrible city."

"Yeah." Bounce had gotten a hundred gold pieces for the ring. Now that he knew what it was, he should have asked for a hundred times that amount.

Gryphilix looked at him for a long moment, but then he seemed to think better of whatever he'd been contemplating and set off into the sky. Bounce settled into the chair and pondered who might have used a sleep spell on Gryphilix. Perhaps there were powerful magic forces on board the coach wagon even now? It would be best to wait for the right time to take care of Dar. Besides, he liked Dar and didn't want to see him killed. *But it is him or me*, Bounce said to himself.

And *me* was always his first choice.

Off in the tower, Letin watched the sun come up. He hadn't slept all night. He couldn't remember some of his spells, and he knew his eyes were red like the morning sky. He listened intently, and before long, he was sure he could hear something stirring next door. After a while the noises became rhythmic, and he knew what was going on. Again.

Letin went over to the chamber pot and dry heaved several times. She knew his feelings. She knew he would suffer upon hearing all of this. He knew she didn't care.

Letin wiped his mouth with his sleeve and went to get a bottle of brown liquid out of the sack next to his bed. He pulled out the cork stopper and took a long draw from it. He could feel his mind starting to sharpen, his body start to rejuvenate. After the whole thing was gone, he felt no need for rest. His spells were still gone, but physically, he felt pretty good. Mentally, he was on fire, his mind racing, thinking of his next move.

He had just about worked out the last detail of his fifth plan when he was sure he heard the door opening next door. He rushed out of his own room, and there was Vulia, fully dressed, heading out on some business errand.

"Hello." Letin figured the less said, the less his true feelings could escape.

"Hello, Letin." She seemed distracted, not really looking at him.

"How did you sleep?"

"Far too little." She grinned a knowing smirk, the flames of their passion twinkling in her eye.

"I heard."

"Really?" She looked at him and for the first time seemed to notice the flatness of his demeanor and the rage that colored his face.

"What about *him*?" He tried to not make his word ooze anger, but it wasn't working.

"I'm done with him." She looked down as she tugged at one of her sleeves, pretending to adjust it. "All looks and nothing else."

"He didn't please you?"

"That is my concern."

"When will we...." He looked at her body, feeling as if it was both unclean and holy at the same time. "Again?"

"That is my concern."

The pause that followed her comment was both long and awkward.

Vulia broke the silence. "We need a better plan for the vessel. And hopefully this idiot's seed will work."

"Unlike mine?"

She snorted a laugh. "Unlike everyone's. I have things to do."

She walked off, leaving the door to her room slightly open. Letin stood at the door for a while but did not open it, formulating a sixth plan. When he finally did walk in, he found Trypia pulling his pants on. He wore nothing underneath them, and seeing him naked made Letin sick to his stomach. The man seemed to be oblivious of his presence—Letin stood for a while and tried to remember a good spell to teach this fool his lesson, but none presented itself. He changed his mind: same plan, different method.

"Hello, Trypia."

Trypia turned and looked at the intruder to his room.

"Oh. Hello, Lesin."

"Letin." He started walking toward Trypia.

"Whatever." Trypia went back to getting dressed. He did not notice how close Letin was getting.

"What did you and Vulia do, Trypia?" Letin fingered the dagger at his waist.

"Last night I enjoyed her twice. Under that robe is a nice, tight body." Trypia turned and looked at Letin. "And I took her again this morning. She is…"

"She is mine." Letin pulled his dagger from its sheath at his belt and, without much grace and with too much force, slashed Trypia's throat. Trypia tried to stem the flood of blood with his hands, but the blade cut deep, puncturing his major artery and windpipe.

"This is what happens to those who stand in my way or take what is mine."

Trypia fell over, staring at Letin with disbelief and fear as the effects of shock started to rob him of any ability to think or react.

"You did both." Letin sheathed the dagger. It had done its job.

Letin then kneeled next to him and watched as the life force ebbed out of his victim. Once the body went limp, he stood up. He started to walk out the door but then suddenly turned and rushed back to the body. He pulled the dagger again and buried it in the body again and again and again. He stabbed it until his robe was covered in blood and the walls of the room ran red.

Letin stood, leaving the dagger where it had buried itself. He walked out of the room and dabbed at his face with a cloth, trying to remove the blood, then he went back into his room and took another robe out of the sack by his bed. After putting it on, he collected his things. One of the items he placed into the sack struck a chord with him. He looked at it for a moment and then lifted it out. He unrolled the scroll. It was a magic spell, and just the one for the moment. With his sack on his shoulder, he started reading it. When he was done, the vellum on which the words had been inked disappeared into dust and a small ball of flame appeared in Letin's hand. He walked next door, threw it at Trypia's body, shut the door, and then walked down the hallway. About fifteen seconds later, the door blasted off its hinges and fire shot in all directions. Letin mumbled to himself, "You did both."

On the plane of ether, the shadow figure watched his disciple. A bit amateurish in his execution of the act, but a good showing nonetheless, he thought. He pondered if his mindwhispering was too effective. Every time he used it, somebody died. A bloody, savage, brutal, violent death.

A delicious event every time.

"My boy," he said, talking to himself, "perhaps you are too evil."

He laughed.

NINE

Sand

No matter how many plans you make, the outcome can escape from you like sand from your hand.

—M'kill the Vicious

For the rest of the day, Gryphilix only came back on oc-casion, and he didn't even stay when the coach wagon stopped for the night. He helped set up the camp and then took off again.

"This really leaves us unprotected," Yspeida commented to Dar as they stood next to the fire and watched Gryphilix fly off into the night sky.

"What do you mean?" Dar rubbed his hands together, trying to keep them warm.

"It means one of us will be on watch alone tonight." She had caught him rubbing his hands. "Mine get cold when I get nervous too."

Dar smiled. "I'm not nervous."

"You're not a very good liar." It was her turn to smile.

"You have no idea." He tried to keep his face straight but wasn't able to do it.

"So, what do you think the schedule should be?"

Dar looked Yspeida in the eye. "I think we should assign everyone with combat experience short shifts. Something like one hour each. That means Drij, you, Knock, Bounce, and I will all take turns."

"You trust the others?" She looked at him with doubt.

"Bounce, I'm not too sure about, but we can put him either first or last so we'll be ready in case something comes up." Dar eyed the rest of the passengers, wondering if any of them could help man the guard.

"It takes me awhile to get to sleep," Yspeida said, "so I can go right before him. I'll probably be just getting to sleep as he ends his shift." She focused her gaze on something, but Dar wasn't paying enough attention to figure out what it was.

Dar decided the rest of the passengers were a lost cause. "And I can go right after him."

Adalia walked up, casket in hand. "I can take a shift too."

Dar looked at her with disbelief. "We need trained people."

"I can yell for help just as loud as the rest of you." Adalia's face was resolute.

Yspeida looked at her and nodded. "It's not like we'll expect the guard to hold everyone off until we have breakfast and a drink, is it?"

Dar looked at Adalia. He knew she wanted to help, but she didn't need to risk herself anymore.

"I really need to do this, Dar," she said, her eyes pleading more than her voice did.

Yspeida turned toward Dar, her hands on her hips. "As one warrior to another, I believe she needs this chance to prove herself."

Dar considered Yspeida's comment for a beat. "She doesn't need to prove herself to me."

"Men." Yspeida put her arm around Adalia. "Always about you." Adalia giggled softly before allowing Yspeida to continue. "She needs to prove it to herself. We all must prove to ourselves what we can do. Men get battles and schools and training, and women get lessons in sowing seeds and sewing clothes. The human heart is hungry for adventure and excitement. She must understand her own limits before she can really live."

Dar listened but wasn't moved. "This isn't the Torrents, and this isn't the High Plateaus. This is a much different world than the one you come from, Yspeida. There is evil everywhere, either by chance or by choice, and it will come. Somebody is after one of us, and Adalia may be the target. Putting her on watch just means she'll be an easier target."

Adalia lost the fun look that the giggle had brought to her face. "I will not disappoint you. I will protect us all." She presented the casket. "I will protect May."

"That seals it," Yspeida started a wry smile. "The shift rotation will be Drij, Knock, Adalia, Yspeida, Bounce, and then Dar. We'll need to go just a little over an hour each, but that won't be a problem. Bounce can get the lizards warmed up during Dar's shift, and then we can hit the road again."

"You seem to be in charge, Yspeida"—Dar could see her start to bristle until he finished his comment—"and it suits you. A lot better than the revenge mission you're on."

"Perhaps you are right." She started to walk off. "Helping others has more honor in it."

Letin walked into the new room where Vulia was staying. She was brushing her hair, once again, while sitting in front of the mirror. She was wearing her favorite silken robe, the one she always wore after a bath.

"I have news about the target."

She looked at him in the mirror but otherwise continued her ritual.

"We can mount an ambush tonight. The traitor will have a shift during the watch, and the winged man is having trouble staying awake, so there will be nobody on guard."

"What assets do we have in the area?"

Letin wrinkled his nose, trying to smell her hair from where he was. "Pretty limited, but I think we can mount a good-sized force of goblins, perhaps some gnolls. We have one gargoyle here in town who we can get there in time for the attack."

"So, you have a plan?" She caught him staring at her hair. She seemed to be able to tell he was having trouble staying focused.

"The goblins and gnolls will try to kill as many as possible as the gargoyle swoops down and snatches the vessel." He held out his hand, maybe just a foot or so away, though he desperately wanted to stroke her hair. To do so without permission would court her fury.

"And the winged man will just let his mortal enemy fly away?"

"I can give the gargoyle my ring of invisibility." She continued to brush her hair. As she finished the stroke, her hand rubbed against the smooth silk of her evening robe. He hoped that she would come to her senses, especially after the Trypia episode, and see that she had been pushing him too hard and she needed to make some amends.

"Put it into motion," said Letin, his voice quivering.

She stopped brushing her hair and stood up. "And when the gargoyle has the casket, you may have your reward." She let the robe fall to the floor, revealing her unclothed body. Letin gasped at the sight of her nakedness, and he fell to his knees.

"Hurry," she purred as she stepped past him and moved onto the bed. "But remember," she chided him as she climbed under the covers, "failure gets you nothing."

"Yes sister." Letin got to his feet and walked out of the room to set events in motion.

Things went like clockwork until finally it was Bounce's turn. He had actually gone and tried to relieve Yspeida early, but she wouldn't have any part of it. Finally, when the chime from Dar's timekeeping device sounded, she handed him a torch.

She looked sternly at Bounce. "You are in charge now. Failure means your death."

"If I wanted to, I could kill all of you in your sleep. I could have done that days ago. I want to see the dawn as bad as you do."

"You might be worthy of trust someday." Yspeida walked over to her bedroll next to Adalia's. "Until then I would make sure that nothing happens. To any of us." She watched the area around the camp for a while before she laid down to sleep.

Bounce completed his normal patrol around the camp. He placed a new log in the fire and walked the perimeter of the light. At each corner he waved the torch back and forth, signaling to whomever Letin and Vulia was sending to take the casket. He'd made about four laps when he saw a dark group of creatures approaching from the far side of his route. He hurried over to that side and waved his torch again. He felt an odd draft and looked up into the night sky. By the light of the torch, he could just barely make out an arc of arrows flying over his head toward the coach wagon. One landed near him—perhaps a warning, perhaps with lethal intent.

Was this a distraction? Was this the force sent by Vulia and Letin, as per his message? Another arrow passed near Bounce—too near. His natural survival instincts kicked in, and he made a decision.

"Alarm! Alarm! All to stations!! We are under attack!!"

Dar roused out of his sleep quickly and pulled Weeper from the pile of equipment near his bedroll. He couldn't immediately see what caused the alarm, but no matter. He knew enough to get near where the alarm had been called from. He had been sleeping in his armor, something he had learned to do at the Fortress of Angels, and he had all his senses about him as he got to where he thought the cry had started.

"*Alegro brilianix.*"

Dar turned to see Drij casting a Continual Light spell, which quickly turned the inky blackness surrounding them into a small area of daylight. Off about a hundred feet away was a band of a dozen goblin archers. They were raining arrows down on the coach wagon, but those arrows didn't make noise when they impacted. In front of them were six gnolls, who appeared to be guarding the goblins from the approach of foot soldiers. The gnolls, being almost a foot and half taller than the goblins, were on one knee, and all watched the goblins firing, lest one of them accidentally take a stray shot in the back. The gnolls were tougher than the goblins, and Dar knew that this was a difficult fight in the making. The effects of the Continual Light spell allowed everyone to see where their attackers were, and it wasn't long before Dar noticed Yspeida make a break for the goblin archers. A hail of arrows forced her to stop and race for cover. Knock joined Dar and Drij as they all did the same.

"We are in a tight spot," Knock started.

"Why is it that everybody always starts with the obvious?" Drij apparently didn't find her comment as humorous as she had intended.

"We still have options." Dar looked around, trying to keep an eye open for what those options might be.

"We need to take out some of those archers. That's the first option we should take." Drij pointed his finger at the little green men off in the distance.

"Oh dearie me, here I went and left my good wand back at home," Knock countered.

"Shut up, you two, and let me even the odds." Dar pulled out Weeper and quickly fired a salvo of six arrows from his magical quiver. He was careful not to select the fat-bodied arrows. Those he needed to save for hard targets, like the Trolls or bridges. Six arrows, three hits, two kills. The rain of arrows didn't seem to slow.

"How do you keep that quiver full?" Drij looked on, and he seemed to be keeping count of the remaining arrows in Dar's quiver.

"Magic," Dar grunted as he let fly another arrow. Four hits, three kills.

Knock nodded. "I've heard of that thing. Infinite Quiver or something like that. Pretty useful, if you ask me."

"It is," Dar agreed. This one was a miss. He leaned back behind the rock he was using for cover and waited for another round of goblin arrows to silently hit the ground. After firing that many arrows so quickly, he figured he should catch his breath and evaluate what was going on. He leaned out to see that Yspeida was safe but vulnerable and the coach wagon had arrows stuck through the skin of its roof but otherwise looked okay. There was a round of arrows sticking out of the back of the nearest lizard, but by the lack of blood, they had failed to penetrate the thick hide of the beast. Dar looked again at the goblins and gnolls. One of the goblins was casting a spell and rubbing its hands against the one Dar had wounded. After a moment the wounded goblin got up and started fighting again.

"They have a shaman." Knock said what Dar was thinking.

"They had a shaman," Dar retorted. He pulled out one of the fat-bodied arrows and let it fly at the spell caster. The arrow flew true and struck the goblin with such force that it flew back almost ten feet. Then the remaining fuel in its shaft caught fire and finished the job.

Dar leaned back behind the protective cover of the stone.

"Knock," Dar said, looking over at her. "You notice something?"

She lifted an eyebrow and scrunched up her face. "Something like what they aren't doing?"

"I don't get it," Drij interrupted. "What do you mean?"

Dar and Knock spoke in unison: "They aren't coming at us."

"So, is that a bad thing?" Drij's eyes darted between Dar and the enemy.

Knock answered. "It means this is just a holding action."

"But holding for what?" Dar wondered aloud as he fingered another arrow.

Adalia watched from behind the coach wagon. The battle seemed to have entered a stalemate. Dar was killing off the goblin archers slowly, but he kept stopping to talk to Knock and Drij. Yspeida seemed awfully exposed in her position, but she hadn't been hit yet. Occasionally an arrow or two would come Adalia's way, but the arc needed to reach her position meant it would hit the roof of the coach wagon first. She watched as Dar shot another salvo of arrows, killing another two goblins. She felt the swirling of the air, like a downdraft of air on her head. Expecting it to be Gryphilix, she turned around, making sure to keep behind the coach wagon. But it wasn't Gryphilix. It wasn't anybody at all. She looked around and saw nothing. She was just about to turn around again when she noticed May's casket starting to float into the sky.

"May!" she yelled out, momentarily forgetting the fact that the casket was empty. She rushed over to the box as it moved around the side of the coach wagon. Fearing it was going to climb into the sky, she flailed at the force holding the box. She hit something that felt like stone and stopped. She was about to hit it again when it hit her. The force of the impact spun her around, and the last thing she saw as she faded out of consciousness was the casket flying off into the night sky.

Dar was just recovering from another round of arrows when he thought he heard Adalia cry out. Knock heard it too, and she crouched like a cat, ready to run to her side.

"One, two." Dar readied a bunch of arrows.

"Three!" Knock yelled as she took off running for the coach wagon just as Dar took his aim. Drij also stood up, trying to distract the archers from the diminutive Knock. Dar went four for four, which caused the number of arrows shot by the goblin archers to just about drop off completely. Knock had nearly made it to the wagon when the last four goblin archers took their aim at the halfling. They were just about to let a salvo fly when Gryphilix came out of the sky and crushed one of their skulls. In a quick, fluid motion, he pulled the morning star from the ground where the goblin had fallen and struck the next archer over in the side of the head, killing him. Dar finished the job with an arrow that pierced the eye of the far archer.

Seeing the new threat, the gnolls stood and rushed at Gryphilix. He struggled to get back into the air and barely escaped the morning stars and swords of the gnolls. Yspeida saw her opening and left the cover behind—Dar watched as she ran, drawing both Hack and Slash. She covered the ground quickly, but the gnolls were smart enough to realize things had turned and formed a defensive circle. It had gone worse than they had realized, and it was their turn to have arrows rain on them. But unlike those of the barely effective goblin archers, Dar's arrows were hitting more often than not, and quickly the six were four and then three. Seeing Yspeida as a close target that would stop the hail of death, they rushed forward and met her halfway.

Dar put away Weeper and drew Winter. Then he took off running.

Knock called out to Drij. "I need help!"

Drij ran back to the coach wagon and quickly scrambled aboard. He found Knock holding Adalia very gently. The limp form of the young maiden was bleeding from a gash on her head, and Knock was struggling to close the wound.

"She is cut badly and needs magical help," Knock told him.

"I might have used all of my powers with that light spell."

"She needs you to find out." Knock looked at him with a kind eye. "You need to find the spell energy. Think not for yourself—think and pray for her."

Drij focused his energy and centered his thoughts. He started a prayer for her, and began his motions for the spell. He had cast it a thousand times before he had joined with the Holy, and he hoped that the selflessness of the act would allow his old gods to save this girl. He promised to return to the old ways if they would just let this one spell come out right.

He chanted the magic phrases and placed his hands on her head. He continued his chant for what seemed like minutes, hoping and praying it would work.

"You can stop," Knock said flatly. There was a little sadness in her voice. Was the girl dead?

Drij opened his eyes. The cloth was away from Adalia's brow, and the wound had closed. Adalia's eyes were open. She said, "I'd like to sit up, Drij, if you don't mind."

Drij released her head and moved back, allowing her to get into a sitting position.

"Whoa." Her head tilted back and forth a little before steadying. "I'm a little lightheaded."

Drij smiled and then went to the rail of the coach wagon to check on the battle outside. He saw Dar and Yspeida—and one of the gnolls encased in ice. The rest of the gnolls were gone, probably dead or running away. He was just about to report the good news when Knock announced the bad news first.

"The casket is missing."

"Good news." Letin barged into Vulia's bedroom. It was closer to dawn than midnight, and she was sleeping alone for a change. He tiptoed up to her and gently caressed her face, and she started to stir. He pulled back the covers, revealing her still naked body. He removed his clothes and jumped in. She was barely awake by the time he finished. He had probably hurt her a little, but he figured at least it was over for her quickly. They both rolled over as they uncoiled their bodies, and he noticed she immediately went back to sleep. He got his first full night's sleep in almost three days.

When Letin awoke, she was already out of the bed, fully dressed and looking out the window. She was struggling to continue a conversation with something outside the open window. Letin knew immediately it must be the gargoyle. He sprang out of bed, still naked, and ran over to the window.

"Do you have it?" He looked the gargoyle in the eye.

The red-eyed beast nodded.

"Why won't he give it to me?" Vulia snapped.

"You're not his master." Letin stuck his arms out the window. "Present it to me."

The gargoyle rose up a bit, reaching for something off the roof. It gently floated back down to the level of the window and presented the box. The wooden casket seemed to float into Letin's hands, and he quickly set it down on the floor of the room.

"The ring too, please," he said without looking away from the casket. A light tinkling noise echoed through the room— the gargoyle had just thrown the ring into the room. Letin was too focused on the box to deal with the insolence right now, but he would make the gargoyle pay. "Sister, shut the window and let us see what we have."

"I agree, Letin. And get dressed." Vulia pulled the heavy curtains, leaving only the flickering light of the various candles in the room to serve as illumination.

Letin grabbed his robe from the floor where he had discarded it and donned it quickly. He would have liked to leave it off and celebrate their glorious triumph with a little private moment with Vulia, but it would wait. History was in the box, and he was one step closer to immortality.

"I'll open it." Vulia was already on her knees, her hands hovering over the box.

"Do it."

Dar, Knock, and Adalia stood around inside the Box looking into the Mirror of Proof. Knock had arranged with Gryphilix to get the room for a short meeting, and the trio was eagerly awaiting news of where the false May had gone. Dar had just finished saying the magic phrase that turned the mirror on. They had placed the ring in the bottom of the box, hoping that whoever took it would put it on. But to their dismay, the doll had been jostled on top of the ring. They would only be able to hear what was happening where the other ring lay.

"Do it."

It was a male voice, familiar, but not one that jumped out at them. Each looked at the others, hoping one of them would recognize the person speaking. It was obvious that none of them did.

There was a creak as the wood of the lid was pried open.

"What?" It was the male voice again.

A female scream echoed through the ring. Dar reckoned it must have been near deafening to be in the same room with her.

There was a scrambling sound as somebody dug around in the casket. Then the sound of what was probably the doll hitting the ground reverberated around the Box.

"I told the gargoyle what to do! I gave him clear instructions. He knew his orders."

The female voice said something that they could not hear.

"It will be done. I know just the place and time."

Then came the sound of the lid being shut, and after a while a crunching sound repeated several times. What sounded like magic words were heard faintly in the distance, followed by the sounds of a crackling fire.

"I think they just burned the casket." Dar looked at Adalia.

"After smashing it," Knock offered.

"They are pretty mad right now." Adalia stood, since the mirror was black now. "They are…"

"I know who they are." Everyone turned. It was Drij, standing over by the door.

"This is a private meeting." Knock started to head over to him, but Dar placed his hand gently on her shoulder.

"And tell me, Drij," he said, "who are they?"

"The man was very clearly that Letin fellow who was here a couple of days ago."

"Letin? The man who was working with Trypia?" Adalia looked at him in disbelief. "Why would he want my May?"

Drij shook his head "I have no idea."

Dar paused for a moment and then offered a better idea. "They want it for a magic jar. They want to put a soul into it."

Knocked gasped but recovered quickly. "Whose soul?"

Dar was going to hazard a guess when the conversation started up from the mirror again. All they could hear was the male voice, and he seemed to be talking to himself.

The night's sleep had left Letin feeling well again. His mind was sharp, but his anger was making it hard to focus.

"For the ninth time, I have failed you, Master." He started to pace around the room. "I will visit you in your Ethereal prison as soon as I am able to finish the spell."

He looked at the mirror. He could still hear her brushing her hair; he could still smell her. He could still feel her. He couldn't fail her again. He couldn't fail his master again.

"How can I be so powerful yet fail so much?"

He collapsed onto the floor and began to cry.

"I have done everything I could. I started the Cabal. I stole from the bellies of their mothers all the babies that were nearly ready to be born I could find. I traveled the whole continent looking for a vessel for my master. I finally find the perfect choice, and then this."

He pounded on the floor. He heard a snicker from the window. It was the gargoyle. His spirits soared—a perfect outlet for his anger. He pulled the curtains, started a quick spell, snapped his fingers, and then pointed at the gargoyle. The gargoyle disintegrated before his eyes. But it wasn't the normal Disintegration spell; it was Letin's own modified version. Instead of being a quick, instantaneous destruction, it was a slow, melting-away process, like being boiled over a low fire. The gargoyle suffered and howled as it melted into eternity.

Letin looked at where gargoyle had been. He looked at the casket. He looked at the mirror. He saw everywhere what his evil had wrought, and how little it had gotten him. His near epiphany stopped there as he picked up a nearby metal candlestick and threw it into the mirror, shattering it into a thousand little shards. The candle stayed lit, and between the fire that claimed the casket and this new fire, it started to spread.

Letin picked up his things and walked out the door.

Vulia's things were not so lucky.

The four of them put the mirror down. The voices where silent, and the only noise they could hear was the crackle of flames and burning timbers. Dar said the magic phrase and turned off the mirror's magic powers.

Adalia broke the silence. "What is an 'Ethereal prison'?"

Dar looked off into the distance, as if trying to see into time itself. He focused and tuned out the world.

Drij answered for him. "I have no idea."

Knock too was stumped. "It is a new phrase to me. I have heard of the Slaver's Prison, the Hellgate Prison, and the Neverprison of the Warrior Lords. Even been into a nameless prison or two. But nothing like that."

They all looked at Dar. He still said nothing. Finally, after what seemed like ten minutes, he turned to Knock.

"I know who will know. Knock, you must keep Adalia safe. Use Yspeida as a bodyguard. Blow your cover if you must, but keep her safe." He looked at Adalia. "Keep the other Ring of Promise on your finger at all times. With it on, I can track you with a Find Object spell. I'm sure this Letin fellow will want to take you alive so you can tell them where May is. Be strong—they might get rough with you."

"I will." She took a deep breath.

"What about me?" Drij looked curious as to what his role would be.

"I need you to come with me. I'll need your help." Dar started out of the Box.

"Where are we going?" Drij asked as he passed through the door.

"To see an old friend."

"Who?"

Dar started to prepare the spell that would be able to carry both of them to the far reaches of Holimoren. He grabbed Drij so he would come too.

"Mrix Trel."

The next thing Drij knew, he was near the land of his fathers, far to the north. They were about three days' walking distance from Magrican, the heart of magical studies for Holimoren. He had been near here as a boy, but he had never seen this place.

"Why couldn't you just teleport us to Redemption?" Drij was furious.

"The spell I used doesn't work that way." Dar sounded oddly calmed. Drij couldn't immediately figure out Dar's location. "The spell only returns me here. We'll have to ask my friend for the way back."

"Friend? Where are we?" The words burst from his mouth.

"Drij, you can't tell me you don't know this area." This time Dar's voice came clear as a bell from behind him. Drij turned to see the largest fortress he had ever seen. Dar said, "Only Harlec Castle is bigger."

"Wow!" was all Drij could get out. He could tell even Dar was impressed.

"Yeah. I said the same thing the first time I saw it." Dar started walking up to the front door. "But wait until you see the inside."

Drij jogged to catch up. Earlier in his trip, this would have caused him to get winded, but now he eased into the fast pace that Dar was setting.

"When were you here last?" Drij asked, trying to drink in the enormity of the structure in front of them.

"You'll hear soon enough. Mrix brings it up every time. But promise me you'll ask no questions of me until we leave."

"What about Mrix? Can I ask him questions?"

"At your own peril." Dar had an impish grin on his face.

"Interesting." Drij paused for a second; Dar wasn't the type to kid around.

Dar reached the front door and grabbed the large knocker it bore. It was shaped like a comet, with the tail reaching back to the hinge. When Dar let it go, the knock was loud enough to hurt Drij's ears. As they stood around, Drij stuck his finger into his ear, hoping to help with the ringing.

"Hello?" The voice came from nowhere, it seemed.

"Hello, Mrix. It is me, Dar. I have come for tea."

"And?"

Dar turned and looked at Drij. "And I have a friend."

"I look forward to meeting them." If the voice hadn't sounded so scary, it might actually have seemed friendly.

A loud metallic clunking noise echoed through the door, and it swung open slowly. Drij stepped back and looked inside the hinge side—there was a large silver gear pushing the door open. The door itself was over two feet thick and was made of solid steel.

"That door must weigh more than a dragon!" Drij said in awe.

"Each door of this structure is fifty tons." The pride of the creator was clear to be heard in the mysterious voice.

"It is a fortress, you know," chimed in Dar. He waited until the door was open enough for two and then charged forward—it was a second before Drij, distracted, realized Dar had already gone in. Following Dar's lead, he dashed inside, and just in time; when the door hit its maximum open point, there came another click and it flew shut. Even back some ten feet from the door inside, Drij could feel the wind and reverberations from it slamming shut.

"I regret that I haven't fixed that door's shutting mechanism yet." It was the mystery voice. Drij turned around and saw a man who had left middle age behind a year or two ago. He was stout—not fat, really, just a well-fed man with a large frame. He had a gentle face with a small graying goatee and short black hair.

"You have come to talk, Dar, as we only ever talk over tea. What's it been, over a decade?"

"How long have you known Dar, sir?" Drij ventured to ask, though he had not yet been introduced. Dar turned and gave him a quick scowl.

"I first hired you to save my daughter, what, about a dozen years ago?" Mrix smiled. "And you left her crying so you could join that wizard's school."

"She never did forgive me, did she?"

"Maybe in another hundred years." Mrix laughed. "I know her mother is still holding a grudge about the time I burned her favorite shoes. And that was three centuries ago."

"So you're an elf, sir?"

"Please call me Mrix. *Sir* makes me sound old. And I'm not an elf, young man." Drij awaited the other shoe. "I'm half-elven. My father was human; my mother was elven. Just like Dar."

That one had Drij reeling.

"Enough chat about me." Dar glanced over at Drij. "I need to know about something called the Ethereal Prison."

It was now Mrix's turn to look stunned. The silence, Drij knew, spoke volumes. They had come to the right place.

"You are dealing with a great evil." Mrix started to walk across the enormous room, and Dar quickly went after him. Drij worked to keep up with their pace.

"There is an ancient tale of a powerful staff," Mrix continued, "a Staff of the Magi that would grant whoever wielded it great power. But it was evil through and through, and if it got into the hands of a weak man, the magic in it would take the man over."

They turned out of the room and into a hallway. It was long hallway, about ten times the size of the coach wagon. At the far end was a set of thick doors about half the size of the fortress's outer doors. Drij figured they were heading deep into Mrix's sanctuary.

"And if it was owned by a strong evil," Mrix went on, "an ego that could withstand its magicks, it would make the both of them stronger, stronger than any wizard alone. The last rumored owner of the Staff of the Magi is probably the one in the prison."

They took a left, then a right, then another left. They passed another set of fortified doors and reached what appeared to be a research wing. Tables were everywhere, each covered with various forms of gears and odd-shaped glass containers. Drij saw a candle that burned with a fiery blue light, which had heated the metal sitting over it until it was red hot. Finally they came to a large set of doors, about twice a man's height. Mrix went over to a small panel next to the door and manipulated whatever type of controls or locks were over there. Then he continued, saying, "If this combination of staff and wizard was about to be bested in combat, the owner could break the staff. The retributive strike would consume all of the magic from the holder and the surrounding area, making the staff act as a focusing lens. The power of the magic would be horrible to behold. It would devastate a huge area."

"Armageddon," Drij whispered. Dar turned—he too appeared to be considering what the ramifications would be if this were if true. The door had finished opening, and beyond it was an enormous library. Millions of tomes lined the walls.

"Yes, young man," Mrix said. "You speak of the legendary final battle in the War of Armageddon. The alleged end of the most powerful and most evil magic user ever to walk Holimoren."

Dar frowned. "Legend was, the destruction consumed him."

Mrix walked over to one of the many desks and reached underneath it. He pulled out a modestly thick tome and laid it down on the desktop. It was titled *The Worst Day in the History of Holimoren.*

"Nice title." Drij's comment drew a wry look from Dar.

"And if the story it contains is true, it's an understatement." Mrix shook his head as he continued, "It tells of a most horrible day. I'm glad to say I've never seen anything that comes close to carnage outlined in this tale."

Mrix opened the book and scanned through pages. Finding what he was looking for, he slowed down and appeared to drink in every word. "It is as I feared," he said. "It appears we are most likely talking about the one who caused the war." He tapped the words on the center of the book. "The entry here calls him Kygger." He snapped the volume shut. "And what your telling me means that he is not dead. He was just transported to the Ethereal plane as part of the retribution strike."

"Kygger? Isn't that a town on the road to Holin? Who is this Kygger?" Drij said softly, afraid to know.

Mrix looked away from the book toward Drij. "There is only a shadow of history on the man Kygger. You'd think the most powerful wizard to ever walk Holimoren—one who conquered from the Baron of the Brown all the way down to deep into the Elven lands—would be remembered. But it seems the gods themselves have flung him from the pages of history. There is only a rumor of one other book about his life and times, and the one entry in this journal from the founder of the Journe…a charitable group. Kygger's history has been scattered across the sands of time the way he himself was scattered across the Ethereal plane after the retribution strike."

"Ethereal plane?" Drij said. His head was hurting, and that pain was probably going to get worse before it got better.

"We exist in a space that is defined by the three linearities," Mrix explained. "There are actually at least five linearities. Well, six if you count time."

"Really?" It was clear Dar was in over his head too.

"Oh yes." Mrix's eyes brightened as he continued, his excitement building. "And from the Astral and Ethereal linearities, or planes, you can reach all the outer planes—the Hells, the Heavens, the Abyss, all of them. Even the elemental planes. From the Astral plane, you can reach the Magic plane. Not that you'd want to—it's just too much for a human mind to compre..." He looked at the pair and stopped. "I've said too much."

Drij suddenly saw things clearly. "But if there are other planes, like the Abyss and the Hells, why don't they count as linearities?"

"A good question." Mrix smiled. "Linearities can coexist. Planes cannot. You can travel the Astral plane or the Ethereal plane and exit straight out into the Prime Material plane in which we live. You will exist in the other three linearities at the same time. We all leave shadows in the Ethereal plane and the Astral too. Well, to a lesser extent."

Dar was getting it now too. "So this Master, as they call him, can see and influence things on this plane?"

"Oh my, yes." Mrix closed the book. "It would look like some sort of ghost, or perhaps come to you in a dream. It could weave its desires into your dreams, but it would sound and feel real. But not real." He wrinkled his eyebrows as he continued. "If you get my meaning. And only at the edge of the Ethereal space. In the deep Ethereal, he'd have no influence on our world."

All the color drained from Drij's face. He knew that moment. "This influence, would you be able to resist it?" he questioned.

"It would sound like your own conscience. Or a god. Or the voice of a god's conscience."

"How do you get back from the Ethereal plane?" Dar asked.

"Well," Mrix replied, "if you have been just visiting from our plane, you'll have a psychic cord that connects your body here on Holimoren to your Ethereal presence. This silver cord, as I call it, must exist for the planes and linearities to stay in synchronization. Without it, you can't come back from the Ethereal plane. You can go to one of the outer planes, like the Hells, without a silver cord, but you can't come back to the Prime Material plane without one."

"So if you had no body on the Prime Material plane," Dar reasoned, "you would need one to take over to come back into this world."

Mrix smiled. "Exactly. Dar, you always were such a fast learner."

Dar patted the older man on the back. "You've always forced me to be."

Drij just stood there, his eyes wide, unblinking.

The coach wagon continued on its steady drive to Redemption. Gryphilix was at the controls, no longer having trouble staying awake. The terrain here was hilly, so he would let the lizards run as fast as they wanted in order to keep enough speed up to conquer the inclines.

But then they came over a rise, and Gryphilix saw the road ahead was blocked by a fallen oak, maybe two. Seeing no way around them, the lizards naturally dug in their claws and resisted the push of the heavy coach wagon as they tried to stop while Gryphilix swore in his native tongue. He turned to yell at Bounce, "Anchor! Bounce! Use the anchor!" He turned forward again and attempted to calculate where the coach wagon would stop. He figured it would about five lengths too far to avoid a crash.

Back at his station, Bounce reached under the rail of the boarding area and pulled a hidden lever. It caused the stairs to come out, and they dragged into the soft clay surface of the road, digging a trench but slowing the coach down faster than the lizards' claws alone. Seeing the "anchor" deployed, Bounce warned the passengers, "Get down; we're going to hit something!"

Everyone scrambled to grab onto something, many of them probably fearing the worst.

Gryphilix removed the food lure that motivated the lizards and locked the controls. He pushed on the brakes, and wood ground into wood, searing the brakes and starting them to smolder. Gryphilix looked at the logs in the road again and then leaped into the air, having done all he could for the coach wagon. It was up to fate and the strength of the lizards now. He climbed higher to see what could be done after the accident.

He was about a hundred feet above the wagon when he saw two hideous gray monsters appear as if out of nowhere and grab onto the coach wagon. They had long, curved talons on the end of long, spindly arms—the combined length meant they almost dragged along the ground. Large, oval, onyx eyes dominated the thin, broad heads that had horns on either side as well as in the middle. Large, birdlike feet connected via double-jointed knees to thick thighs. Chitinous body segments reinforced the notion that they were not of this plane. Both beings reached out with their talons and took hold of the wagon. With strength beyond this existence, the combined force of the two stopped the wagon dead. Gryphilix watched as the fierce-looking creatures boarded the coach wagon and started throwing people off of it. He could hear the she-warrior attack, and he saw her fly out of the coach. The halfling followed suit, sailing out of the wagon face first. He heard a shriek, and then all was quiet.

By the time Gryphilix reached the ground, it had only been maybe two minutes since he'd taken off, but so much damage had been done. He landed next to the halfling, who was starting to roll onto her back. Her arm was bent at a horrible angle, and blood was already welling up into a bruise on her neck.

"You're hurt pretty badly," he told her. "You need to hold still."

Knock looked at him like he was from another reality. "Are they gone?"

Gryphilix turned quickly and looked. "Yes, they are gone."

"Mezzodaemons." She lay back in shock.

"Don't you worry..." Gryphilix tried to set the wound and placed her legs so that her knees were in the air. "I've got a potion or two that will set you right."

He got up and ran over to the coach wagon. The lizards had collapsed under the strain—or perhaps passed out from the shock of seeing such vile creatures. He got to his control seat and lifted it up into the air. Several small potion skins were all at the front, pushed by their momentum to one side. He grabbed all of them and ran back. He was just about to the halfling when he saw the she-warrior. She had been unable to get her hands in front of her and hit a patch of gravel off to the side of the road. She had blood flowing from her face and chest and was trying to stand, but the blood was flowing into her eyes, which clearly made it hard for her to orient herself. Gryphilix knew she would bleed to death trying to stand up if he didn't do anything, so he tossed a potion to the halfling and then ran to she-warrior.

When he reached her, he forced one of the potions down her throat. At first she didn't fight him, too dazed to resist. Finally, the first draught started to work, and as she gained some sense, she started to struggle against him. He used his superior strength to finish dumping another potion into her mouth. The bleeding stopped, but it was clear she was still quite weak. She started to speak, but nothing would come out. He turned and ran back to the halfling. He repeated with her what he had with the she-warrior, but Knock didn't respond to the treatment right away. He poured another potion down her throat and then took a listen to her belly. He could hear a fizzing noise.

"Internal injuries," he said, mostly to himself. "My potions might not be enough." He was down to three potions.

"I'll survive," Knock said weakly and then closed her eyes again.

Gryphilix took her at her word and went back over to the she-warrior. The potions had helped her. She was still covered in blood, but it was drying, and no new blood could be seen. Her skin was repairing itself as he watched, but she would still be lightheaded.

"Sit down," he told her.

"What was that?" she asked.

He knew the look on her face as she spoke. He had stayed in the sky rather than face the scaly horrors, some nine-foot-tall nightmares come to life. She had pulled both blades and done nothing but nearly got killed.

"The halfling said they were demons or something," he told her.

"I…" She struggled to stand then decided to lie down. Gryphilix had seen the look on her face many a time; for her, everything hurt.

Gryphilix looked at her for a second before walking away. "I'll be back."

The rest of the passengers who had been thrown out of the coach were all dead, and had most likely died before they'd landed. The ones who had been lucky and stayed in the coach survived. Three people were missing. Judging by the blood on the ground, two were probably bitten or eaten and therefore probably already dead. The last one was the young Adalia. Gryphilix looked, but there was no blood near where he had last seen her.

He then noticed Bounce walking, dazed, and mumbling something about "a deal." Gryphilix was going to ask him about it when Bounce dropped to his hands and knees and vomited.

Some other time maybe.

TEN

Redemption

If you are going to the little town called Redemption, it is best to come either with a clean soul or a well-armed body.

—*Alix Dee'lee's Traveler's Guide to Holimoren*

Nighttime was coming across Holimoren. Mrix offered Dar and Drij lodgings for the night, but only if they promised to stay in the visitor's wing. Dar did his normal nighttime routine of stretches and spell studies, but Drij just sat there. Once that was all complete, Dar decided to look into the mirror and see if there was anything new he could figure out from each of the Rings of Promise. First he viewed the one they had put into the box in which the fake May had been placed. The ring was on a person, someone he didn't recognize. Since there was enough light to see, he scanned around the image. It was a worker digging out the fiery remains of a building. He could make out enough details to see it had been a large fire, probably set by magic, judging by its size.

Then he tuned the magic of the mirror to let him see Adalia.

It was pure black.

Dar watched the mirror for a while, but it was no use. The image wouldn't change. She was alive, but he couldn't see anything. He started a spell and used the mirror to focus the power. By the end of the four-hour chant, he would know where she was. (Well, at least within an hour's walking distance or so. Even magic had its limits.) Drij still wasn't coming out of the funk he had entered into when he heard of the story of Armageddon. Dar was worried about him, but he knew Adalia was in worse shape.

He hoped Yspeida and Knock weren't in trouble too.

Gryphilix held a lonely vigil over the wounded and dead. He wasn't sure if the demons would be back, and he knew he would be their next victim if they did return. But he knew he had to stay, especially since Knock had teetered near death for most of the night. A weaker soul would have already perished, but she fought death off. Gryphilix committed the last of his potions to her and tried to set her arm as best he could. He built a bonfire as night continued to spread its inky blackness around Holimoren. The survivors gathered around to listen, to talk, and to try to make some sense of this madness.

"Does anyone know what happened to the missing three?" Gryphilix spoke in a low tone, but he knew he could be heard by all.

"I saw what happened," Bounce said, still looking nauseous. "They ate the heads of two people and then slung the bodies over their shoulders. They grabbed that woman with the box and then disappeared."

"Was Adalia, the woman with the box, alive?" Yspeida's strength was coming back, but her desire for revenge clearly outpaced her body's ability to function.

"Yeah," Bounce replied. "They used a spell or something to knock her out, but she looked okay." He looked into the fire as if hoping to burn the visions from his mind.

They sat in silence for about ten minutes. Gryphilix couldn't take it any more, so he sauntered over to the logs and started to move them. Bounce took the cue from his master and loped over to tend to the lizards. After that he dug out the stairs and retracted them.

Yspeida just stared at the fire, revenge in her eyes.

Letin lay stretched out on the plush bed. This one was larger than normal, as was the smile on his face. He had gotten the whore who had birthed the vessel, and it wouldn't be long before she cracked under his pressure. That meant the vessel's location would be theirs, and then the Master could return.

If only Vulia would stop doing her business so she could celebrate with him. At what point was it a cover story and when did it become a real job?

"You look happy." As if on cue, Vulia entered the room, in a long, flowing robe with a hood large enough for two people. She start to take it off by pulling it over her head, and Letin hoped she would be naked underneath.

He couldn't have been more wrong. She was wearing armor.

The armor was a thick, black, leather suit with thin metal wires sown into the larger sections on the chest and legs. It curved around her body tightly, leaving little to the imagination. As armor for an assassin, it was perfect. It was silent, seemed to absorb light, and offered protection against most thrusting and stabbing weapons.

"I am ecstatic." He sat up in the bed. "This plan went off flawlessly. We have the mother of the vessel, and she should be conscious now, so the influencing of her can begin. What makes you put on your work clothes?"

She turned and said, anger in her tone, "I can't believe you summoned demons. Now they are rampaging through the area. They are frightening my followers, and I…"

"Wait." He stood up. "Your followers? They follow the word of our master. They are *his* followers."

"You know what I meant. They are attracting attention. You were sloppy, and now you're putting things at risk."

"I'm sloppy?" He moved closer to her. "You're the one running around to all these temples. You're the one who can't bother to help out with the plan. You're the one fooling around with dumb idiot pawns that set us back. You're the sloppy one."

"That's what this is about? That Trypia fellow?" She took a step back. "He's the least of your concerns."

"I know. I killed him." Letin looked at her with contempt.

"He wasn't the only other one, you know." She returned his look.

"And I will kill all of them too."

"Still won't make you any better, little man."

Letin swung to slap her with the back of his hand, but she deftly dodged out of the way and grabbed his arm, which she bent around behind him. He tried to move and pivot out of the hold, but she was stronger than he—and trained to kill.

"You forget, I'm not just trained in the art of magic, brother. I could snap your neck right now and finish this myself."

"You don't have the guts," he told her. "You've taken the coward's way out these last several years. You've let me do all the dirty work. There might be blood on your soul, but never on your hands. Since you formed the Holy, you've lost the focus of the true purpose of our mission."

She pushed on him, closing her arm down on his windpipe, which made it harder and harder to breath.

"You know how many vile and disgusting men I have let into my bed, trying to make a vessel for the Master?" Even with her mouth just a short distance from his ear, her words built into a yell. "I let you defile me on a regular basis, and frankly, I grow sick of it. I have killed, I have sacrificed, and I have worked dangerous jobs for little money to pay for your training at Magrican." Her tone went soft. "You only have power because I gave it to you."

An unsettling level of apprehension was building in Letin. He couldn't breathe, and she wasn't letting up.

"Feeling the panic yet? Nice, isn't it? That's the feeling I get when you lay on me in one of your crude moods, getting your pleasure." She tightened her hold a little. "What about your sacrifices, Letin? What about sacrificing for my needs? I need the Holy. They need me. The Master needs me. The Master will use the Holy to rebuild Holimoren in his image."

Letin made a gurgling sound; she eased up a little and shifted the hold. She was now cutting off not the oxygen to his lungs but the blood to his head. The sleeper hold would put him out in about a minute. He was already woozy, and she was supporting most of his weight.

"Imagine what happens when the God of the Holy, the legend in the Book of Truth, comes to life. A god walking the land! People will flock into the Holy—our master will rule them, and I will be queen."

She tightened her hold on his throat again, and he knew he was about to pass out. "And you'll still be the fool, Letin."

As he fell to the ground, she kicked him in the groin, but the pain faded into the blackness of unconsciousness.

Drij wasn't sure what had happened. He remembered Mrix chanting some magic power phrase for a few beats, and then the next thing he knew, he was standing outside, next to a stone fence. The fence was only two feet high and did little to block the way.

"Where are we?"

"Redemption." Dar spoke without looking at Drij.

Drij looked around. The town that had been his destination on this trip was on the other side of a road; the small fence screened off the road from the field beyond. There was another fence of the same size on the other side of the road, beyond which the buildings of the town stood, made of stone. Everything in Redemption, he knew, was made of stone. Drij looked down and saw he was standing on a piece of stone. The longer he looked at it, the more restless he felt.

It was a tombstone.

"We are in a graveyard!" Drij bolted to the fence. He considered jumping it but waited for Dar to lead the way.

"Everything outside of the Wards is probably going to be a tomb, either marked or unmarked."

"The Wards?" Drij eyed the area around him.

"The town fathers of Redemption got tired of visitors just burying people anywhere, so they established laws as to where they could be buried. Within the bounds of these fences, called the Wards of Redemption, it is illegal and immoral to bury the dead."

"So there are no tombs inside of Redemption proper?"

Dar gave Drij the smallest of smiles. "Just one."

"The founder of the city?" Drij felt like the whole town had an aura of sadness about it.

"Good guess. But wrong."

"Who?"

"The founder's wife." Dar jumped over the fence and started to walk to the town center. "As for the dead, as long as you're walking on the grave by accident and you mean no harm, they won't haunt you. Respect is what the dead look for, really."

"That's comforting." Drij jumped over and caught up to walk beside Dar. "Any other rules I should know about?"

Dar shot Drij a sidelong glance. "Let me do the talking. Remember to not touch anybody, since they are probably dying. Be as calm as you can and keep your wits about you."

"Okay." Drij nodded. He scanned the area; it seemed like the town was pretty empty. "Why don't people use spells to heal the sick?"

"Tradition states that if you come to Redemption while still living, you cannot accept the help of others outside of your family. If your family could have healed you, they would have probably done so at home."

"That's a horrible tradition."

"I agree. But you don't come to Redemption looking to live. You come here looking to die." Dar shot Drij a wistful glance.

"I have been thinking about that." Drij looked forward, not wanting to look at Dar or his reaction. "I think I finally understand what happened that night, and I want to atone for it, not succumb to it."

"That's good to hear." There was joy in Dar's voice.

"I think that fellow from the Armageddon battle had a hand in it."

There was a heavy pause. "And if he didn't?"

"Then I guess I did come here to die." Drij looked at Dar with a new sense of purpose. "But until I know, I choose life."

The two walked in silence until they had reached the middle of town. A typical village square, it was lined with shops of all sorts. On the signpost of one of the buildings was a gold crown. Dar pointed at the sign, and they proceeded to the door. But before they could get there, it opened up and a stout fellow burst out into the square.

"Radby is the name. I'm the Right Honorable Lord Mayor of Redemption." He extended his hand. Dar took it firmly and shook it.

"Lord Mayor."

Drij offered his hand. The Lord Mayor looked at it.

Dar cleared his throat.

Drij put his hand down.

The Lord Mayor put his hand out. Drij took it and shook it.

"The pleasure is all mine, Lord Mayor. I am new to Redemption, and I am learning your ways—I meant no disrespect."

"None taken, my boy."

Drij looked at the Lord Mayor. He was probably five years younger than himself, and his body was almost a perfect sphere. "Thank you, Lord Mayor."

"You boys aren't here to raise trouble, are you?" the Lord Mayor asked. "You both look too healthy to be visiting Redemption for the normal purposes."

Drij began to say something, opening his mouth, but then remembered the rules and shut it; the Lord Mayor just looked at him.

Dar jumped in, saying, "We are looking for a lost person."

The mayor wrinkled his brow. "Missing person? Did this person come looking for purity?"

Dar leaned in so only the three of them could hear. "Kidnapping, actually."

"Never!" The Lord Mayor feigned shock. "The horror of it all."

"And I know the Lord Mayor would never allow such villainy to happen in his noble town, so some vile presence must be lurking in the shadows."

"I know of no evil work in this town." His eyes wouldn't meet either Drij's or Dar's.

Dar stared at him with such intensity that Drij started to feel sorry for the Lord Mayor. Then Dar leaned in closer still and lowered his voice. "Listen, Radby, if I find the person I'm looking for, and I find out you knew she was here the whole time, you'll pay. So help yourself and level with me."

The Lord Mayor seemed about to chastise Dar for his insolence when his face showed that he knew he was outplayed. He replied, crestfallen, "The Church of the Holy."

"What about it?" Drij asked without permission. Dar looked at him and narrowed his eyes slightly.

"Redemption was attacked by two demons over the last couple of nights." The Lord Mayor started to look pale, as if the attack was still happening in his mind. "They attacked several people, biting off their heads and eating them in the middle of the street. After assaulting six or seven people, they wandered into the Church of the Holy, and they didn't come out until the next night."

Dar looked around the square. "This wasn't like demons. They were probably daemons. There is a subtle difference, Lord Mayor, though most people can't tell them apart. Demons are chaotic and evil; daemons are always evil but sometimes organized. Demons respect no one—they wouldn't have rested until the town and the area around it was dead and burning. Daemons would respect a more powerful force—and would follow orders if the reward was great enough. Orders such as heading back to the church." Dar completed his scan of the area and looked at Radby. "Are they still there?"

"I hope to the gods they are not." The rotund man's voice was starting to wane.

Drij could tell that the Lord Mayor was about to bolt. Dar placed his arm on the rotund man. "Where is the Church of the Holy?"

"Next to the Ward opening to the Field of the Chosen." Dar released the Right Honorable Radby, who waddled off as fast as he could back into the stone building from whence he came.

Dar turned duskward and took off at his fastest walking speed. Drij went off after him.

"What is the Field of the Chosen?" Drij asked.

Dar pulled out Winter. Drij could feel the air chill around him.

"Some of the fields around the town are selected by some trait or another to only be the resting area of those that fit its criteria. There is the Field of the Blessed, full of religious leaders and other people of special religious notoriety. The Field of the Chosen is for those of secular power who were great in leadership, politics, or academics. The Field of Honor is for the great generals and the finest warriors. The Field of Power is for magic users."

"No field for the thieves and powerful criminal lords?"

"There is rumored to be a Field of the Damned, but I have never seen it." Dar lifted an eyebrow. "My guess is that Gliindr has."

"Gliindr?"

Dar sighed. He seemed to have forgotten that Drij had never been to Redemption before. "Gliindr is a dwarven warrior who runs the teams of diggers that bury the dead around Redemption."

Drij had never seen Dar move with this sense of urgency. He was struggling to keep up without jogging. Even with his lither body, this was a challenge, but the discussion made him want to keep pace with Dar. "A dwarf?" he asked.

"Dwarves don't believe in the notion of Redemption. They believe that the only way to redeem oneself is by action and work. So being around Redemption doesn't bother them."

"But I thought dwarves only dug for gems and precious metals."

"What do you think Gliindr is looking for? Redemption is sitting on major veins of gold, silver, and gems. But the traditions say that the only time you can dig around here is to bury the dead. No mining is allowed."

Drij thought things over while he used a burst of speed to catch up to Dar. "So they dig holes for the bodies and keep what they find in the process. How deep can they go?" Drij was looking at Dar, not at the road.

"Later," came the terse reply.

"Why?" Drij cocked his head to one side.

When Dar failed to reply, Drij looked up and saw a large square building in front of them—no windows on the first story, several on the second floor, and only one large iron door. Unlike the rest of the town, which was made of sandstone, the building was made of slate. It gave the building a dark, foreboding quality.

"We're here."

Some fifty miles away, the coach wagon was back on track, heading for Redemption. Yspeida held Knock and tried to do what she could for her. Knock was not recovering very quickly, and her arm was still out of alignment, but her strength was building. Yspeida had only felt this powerless once before—she'd hated the feeling then, and she hated it now.

"I'm a she-warrior! I don't fear death!" she yelled to the wind rushing over the driver's seat and into the cabin of the wagon. "Why couldn't they have slaughtered me?"

Knock opened her eyes and tried to smile. "Fate isn't particular about who it changes or how it influences the world. It just does what it needs to do."

Yspeida leaned over and found her tender voice. "How are you doing, my sister?"

"I am glad to say I have been worse." Knock closed her eyes and took a shallow breath. "But sad to say I have been better."

Now that Knock was awake, Yspeida couldn't contain the news any further. "Adalia was stolen by the creatures, and Dar and his companion have not yet returned."

"Dar and Drij have no way to know of the events of today." Knock looked at the gentle flutter of Yspeida's hair in the draft. "Yesterday? I am ill."

"We will be in Redemption in a couple of hours," Yspeida reassured her. "Once Gryphilix got the road cleared of the trees, they started up the lizards again. Ran them cold for a while. It was pretty slow. But Gryphilix figured a way to get them warm. He poured hot water onto a blanket and then put the blanket on them."

"He's a nice man." Knock was clearly trying to be pleasant, but the strength of her pain made it come out sickly and pathetic.

"We can get you treatment in Redemption."

Knock could only reply in a whisper, "No, you can't."

"Why?"

"Redemption doesn't allow healing except by members of the same family."

"Do you have any family?" Yspeida asked, tilting her to the side slightly.

Knock took a deep breath, and it was clear that it really hurt. "No. I probably broke a couple of my ribs too."

The she-warrior leaned over and rubbed her friend's good arm gently. "I thought halflings were pretty stout people."

Knock tried to laugh, but after the first chuckle she had to stop and just smile. "Since I might not make it, and since I doubt you would hurt me in my current state, I guess a small dose of the truth is due."

"Hurt you? I called you *sister*." Yspeida was offended that Knock could even think such thoughts.

"Hear me out." Knock closed her eyes and took a slow, purposeful breath. She held it for a moment then let it out slowly as she spoke. "I am not a halfling. I am an elf. I pose as a halfling to fit into the human nations better."

Yspeida gasped. "I have never seen an elf before. I thought you all hated humans since the Elf Killer War."

"I could say the same about humans." A wry grin was chased by twinge of pain that got Knock back on to her point. "Living like and around others is a sure way to build tolerance and understanding."

They sat in silence for a moment—it was clear that Knock wasn't sure how Yspeida would take her revelation. Most humans reacted to elves with fear. But Yspeida just started to gently rub Knock's head to reassure her.

"I called you *sister*, and I stand by it," was all she said.

It was all she needed to.

Knock smiled. But there was something in that smile that made Yspeida wonder if there was more to come.

Vulia and Letin stood in the center of a magic pentagram. The gate had just finished closing, and the dust that rose up when the portal opened was starting to settle on the slate floor. Vulia leaned over and blew out the candles on the floor. Letin limped to the center of the room, still sore and swollen from his earlier run-in with her foot. They had said barely a word. But the Mezzodaemons had been dispatched back to their infernal plane of origin, and the cost hadn't been too great.

"We could have used them." Letin pouted.

"Shut up. I don't need your back talk." Vulia picked up another candle and held it like she meant to throw it. "Unless you need another lesson."

"I said I'm sorry, Vulia." He winced as he moved forward. His potion of healing had stopped the bruising, but the soreness would linger a couple of hours longer. "I'll be more of a partner."

"We need to get the information out of the prisoner." She lowered the candle, her face softening slightly. "In a short time, this area will be full of people looking for her and the daemons, and we need to have freed the Master by then."

"My scrying has foretold of an eclipse in two weeks." Letin used his foot to break up the pentagram's shape. "My studies have shown that an eclipse could cause massive storms in the near Ethereal plane. That could force our Master out of our reach. We must extract the information we need well before then."

"I'll leave that to you." She left a couple of candles at the corners of the pentagram on the floor, a look of frustration on her face. "I need to attend a meeting of the Holy." She turned and looked at Letin. "Unless you have a problem with that."

"No, my love."

"Don't call me that." She walked out.

After extinguishing the rest of the candles, Letin too walked out of the storage-room-turned-return-gate where they had sent their Daemon minions back home. But instead of turning left like Vulia had, he turned right and went down a set of stairs to the dungeon. He ran his hand along the wall, which was about waist high. Suddenly his fingers dipped into a hidden nook in the wall. He stopped, pushed up with his fingers, and waited for the door to open. Once it did, he walked in and shut the door behind him. A single candle holding a lonely vigil kept the room from total darkness, and it was just enough for him to see the sealed door at the other end of the chamber. Letin walked over to the door and pulled back a heavy leather gasket. Then he opened the door.

Inside was Adalia.

She was floating upside down inside a magic sphere of darkness. Letin would wait for her to fall asleep, and then he would talk to her, trying to implant suggestions into her sleeping mind. He had removed her underclothes to serve as a warning that violence would be next if she didn't cooperate. But Vulia had caused enough damage to scuttle that plan. He would use magic to gain his information. And if she didn't cooperate, he could use more powerful magicks to make her talk. Of course, if he did that, she wouldn't have a brain left, but that wasn't his problem. She came out of her light sleep as he finished his spell, which took effect immediately.

"Tell me what I want to know." He kept his voice flat and even.

"I won't." Her tone matched his.

"I can kill you."

"I know."

"I can hurt you." He voice lowered slightly this time.

"I know."

"I can rape you." Letin almost growled this threat out. He started to get aroused at the thought, but his bruises started to hurt.

"I know." She shifted slightly, as if fighting the spell. He paid it no mind.

"All of that and more will happen if you don't tell me what I want to know."

"I will tell." Her tone remained flat and emotionless, the effect of the Truth spell.

Letin smiled. There was nothing magic couldn't do in his hands. And once he combined his powers with the knowledge of the Master, he would be the greatest magical power ever.

Then he would have his revenge. And the list of targets was long.

"Where is the vessel? Where is the baby?"

"May is in the chest."

"Where is the chest?" Letin got up close to her, so close he could feel her breath on his skin.

"In the closet."

"Where is the closet?" Letin closed his eyes and enjoyed the closeness of her.

"I don't know."

"What do you mean, you don't know?" He opened his eyes and moved away.

"Dar never told me where the magic closet went to."

Closet of Xio! Letin cursed to himself. No wonder they hadn't found the vessel in the course of his scrying. It wasn't on this plane anymore.

"Will you do as I say?"

"I will obey." Adalia's tone remained flat and emotionless.

As much as he wanted to use the Truth spell's commanding force to satisfy his sexual appetites, it was clear he needed it for something else.

Dar got to the front door of the Church of the Holy and sized it up. It appeared to be heavy and thick, and he wondered if it was locked. If it was, he would need some serious magic to open it.

"It won't be locked this time of day," Drij blurted out. "The third Offering of Truth is going to be happening shortly."

Dar tried pushing the door. It creaked but gave way and opened slightly. Not wanting to attract a lot of attention, he quickly stepped inside. Drij seemed more confident, walking briskly to the inner sanctum. Dar quickly recognized Drij's upper hand in this situation and ducked in behind him.

"Put your weapon away." Drij keep his eyes forward. "This is a holy place, and weapons are not allowed to be displayed. You're in my world now, so follow my lead."

Dar nodded before adding softly, "I agree."

They walked into the inner sanctuary, which Dar saw was just like most other churches. Row after row of pews faced the marble altar. Instead of a massive statue of the god or goddess to whom the church was dedicated, the idol was a book, the Book of Truth.

Dar could see that Drij knew the methods of worship, their rituals, but there was something in the way he moved, the way he swiveled his head suggested that he felt out of place here. They took a seat toward the back, near the center aisle, away from the odd collection of what appeared to be a handful of villagers and lower-level priests. "Keep your head down," Drij said as they took their seats, "and once the service is over, we can look around more. Wait for the High Priest to walk down the aisle marking the end. That will be our cue."

"When…" Dar couldn't finish the thought. A small chime rang, and Drij held up his hand. Drij then tilted his head over in deference to the High Priest as they entered the room.

"Followers of the Master, Brothers of the Holy, welcome to the Redemption order of the Holy. I am the Founder—*the First*."

Drij and Dar turned to look at each other. They both recognized the voice but couldn't place it. This wasn't any priest, this was *the* priest—the highest in the Holy, and they'd happened to run into him. The thick black robes covered any trace of his face, so Dar couldn't tell his age or what he looked like, but the man's voice sounded oddly effeminate.

Dar was preparing himself to focus ahead and wait out the sermon when Drij jumped up and ran for the stage. The High Priest had just turned around to grab a container of incense and didn't see Drij coming. But rather than attacking the priest the way Dar thought he would, Drij stopped short and touched the person on the shoulder.

Then he pulled off the hood.

Long blond hair spilled out from underneath it, and the lower-order priests and congregants gasped, a sound that echoed throughout the church.

"Vulia!" Drij yelled.

Vulia pushed the attacker away and looked around at the people in the room. As her eyes landed on each group, she saw a different thing: In some of the priests she saw hatred, desire, and betrayal. In the eyes of the faithful, she saw confusion, and in the eyes of the few female parishioners, she saw a profound sense of respect. She ended at the priests on the stage with her, since they were the closest—one seemed to be reaching for something.

So Vulia reached underneath her robe and pulled out a throwing knife. "First to make a move becomes a martyr."

She needed to shed the robe; it would only hinder her during the combat she knew was coming. She unbuttoned the large wooden buttons with her left hand and let the robe drop, revealing her black, form-fitting leather armor.

"You all disgust me." She took a step back. "When you all thought I was a man, you took the word of the Master from my mouth like a man lost in a desert takes water from an oasis." Another step back. "But suddenly I'm some leper, some vile creature?"

"The Book states that women aren't to be trusted! You're a nothing but a whore!" This came from a rotund priest near the back. He was the one who had the look of desire in his eyes, which had only become more intense with the removal of the robe.

Vulia let fly the knife, and it hit the man right in the neck. Blood immediately began to flow. He let out a scream and collapsed to the floor.

"Drij! Get down!" Dar realized Vulia was starting to cast a spell. Assassin's armor, spells of the magi, and the profession of a cleric? She was a tricky creature.

Dar pulled out his Dagger of the Wasp and prepared to throw it. But before he could, darkness descended over the church. Dar couldn't make out his own hand in front of his face, let alone somebody over a dozen feet away and probably moving.

He countered with a Light spell, but it did nothing. He pondered for a moment. If Vulia had cast Darkness, his Light spell should have countered it. Even if she had cast Continual Darkness, it would have flickered light before going pitch black again.

"Drij! Are you there?" he called.

"Dar, I'm right where I was when the darkness hit. What is it?"

"Some sort of new spell. I cast Light, but it didn't work."

"That's odd." Drij paused before Dar heard from him again. "I just tried blinking repeatedly, hoping it would clear my vision, but I still see nothing.

"I don't even see the light from the sun outside," Dar said. "That is powerful magic."

"Get to the door and see if you can open it."

Dar fumbled around for a few minutes before running into a pew and falling over. He struck his head on the next pew over and lay on the ground for a moment.

"That sounded like you hitting a pew and then hitting the ground."

Drij's attempt at comedy missed the mark. Dar rubbed his head, hoping to make the pain, and Drij's joke, go away. "Drij, what if instead of Darkness, she cast Blindness?"

"Cure Blindness would do it."

Drij was right. Dar sat up and concentrated on the curative spell. He still had enough magical energy to cast it—and leftovers after that too. A minute later the spell was completed.

It was still dark.

"No good. Cure Blindness didn't do it."

The room went silent. Everyone appeared to be thinking over their next move.

A gurgling sound broke the silence. The priest Vulia had attacked was dead.

"Curse this darkness," said a voice in the inky black.

"It's all in your head," came another voice.

"That's it!" Dar shouted.

"I don't get it." Drij said.

"It's an illusion. We are under a spell that makes us think we are seeing black. We are not blind, and our eyes still work fine. There is light in the room. Our minds are being told by the spell not to see any of it."

"She's an illusionist?" Drij sounded really confused.

Dar ignored the question and started his Dispel Magic spell. It would break up the illusion and hopefully let them head after her in pursuit. But it would take some time and use almost all of his remaining magic power for the day.

Vulia had left the main floor of the temple and was heading down the stairs when she heard the sound of somebody tripping over a pew. She chuckled but quickly remembered how much trouble she was in. She kept running for the secret area—and Letin.

How he would gloat!

Maybe it was better to fight off the people above.

Second thoughts aside, she pushed on and quickly reached where she knew Letin would be.

The torture room.

He had constructed it all himself, mostly by using magic, and he'd given it a great deal of attention. She'd always been impressed by its simplicity and how quickly it had broken people. Like the Librarian of Magrican, who'd told them where the secret tomes about their master were located. She hoped Letin's spells and devices had managed to extract the location of the vessel. With the Master's power at her side, she could rule the Holy as a woman openly and without shame.

"Letin?"

"Vulia." He sounded embarrassed.

Vulia rounded the corner of the room, and there was Letin with Adalia in front of him. She was on her knees, and he was just pulling down his pants.

"You sick idiot." She pushed him aside and helped Adalia up. "We need to get out of here. You're supposed to be getting the location of the vessel out of her, not meeting your own pathetic needs."

"Thanks to the damage you did me, I wasn't sure I was still working, so I thought I'd find out." He finished drawing up his pants. "Besides, I have the location. We can safely leave the temple. No need to bring her."

Vulia pulled another dagger and prepared to strike Adalia with it. Adalia made no move to protect herself.

Letin grabbed Vulia's hand. "That isn't necessary either." Vulia gave him a crazed look. "You'll understand soon enough."

Letin started a Teleport spell, and in a wink both he and Vulia were gone.

As Dar finished the final part of the spell, it was as if a curtain had been drawn and the light of the sun was allowed to flow in. Everyone could see—in fact, because of his Light spell, it was a bit bright inside the church. But because the magic had only been working on people's brains, their eyes were already adjusted to the light conditions.

Drij walked up to Dar. "Okay, Dar, now what?"

"We need to figure out where she went." Dar eyed the church, watching the fleeing followers.

"Can you use magic to scan for Adalia?" Drij too seemed to be looking over the flock for signs of foul play.

"I'm pretty low on magic power right now," Dar said just above a whisper, trying to keep any foes from hearing.

"You don't think she was going to kill Adalia, do you?" Drij started to look around.

"Excuse me?" A thin priest came over to Dar. "Are you looking for somebody?"

Dar turned to face the man. He was gaunt and weary looking. Dar could tell he was sick, most likely from the consuming disease. It would eat a man from the inside out. "We are. A woman, probably a prisoner."

"She would be down in the basement." He coughed with a deep, hollow tone.

"Black-lung disease?" Dar thought back to his own father.

"True enough. I came to Redemption to wait for my death and joined the Holy to try to earn a spot in the Heavens."

"You earn that through your actions, not your church." Drij put his hand on the fellow's shoulder. He couldn't have been more than thirty years old.

He stared off into the distance, his eyes full of a haunting sadness. "I know that. Now. But it is too late for me."

"It is never too late." Drij smiled at the man.

The man ignored this, saying, "The way down is over behind the last curtain in the back area of the office. Third door on the left."

Dar reached into his knapsack and pulled out a potion.

"Drink this—it will help with the pain."

"Only the pain of my body. The pain of my soul never will heal."

Drij patted him on the shoulder. "Yes it will, my son. Yes it will."

The two turned and walked toward the stairs down. As Drij reached the top of the stairs, Dar noticed him pause before heading down.

"What's going on?" Dar inquired.

"He took off his robe, and some of the color returned to his face."

"He's still going to die, but all least he's going to feel less pain," Dar lamented.

"His soul will too." Drij wiped away a tear and followed Dar down.

ELEVEN

Hallowed

"The three parts of honor are truth, bravery, and kindness. Hold these things sacred; at least until they get in the way."
—King Albacas the Fourth

Yspeida and the rest of the passengers on board the coach wagon held their breath as the Wards appeared, marking the outskirts of Redemption and the end of their journey. For some it was a final stop—for others it was just a place to sleep for a while before the coach wagon continued on to Novassadra and the other points duskward. For Knock, it would be a chance to heal.

Hopefully.

Yspeida knew it would be the place where she would find her destiny—either by slaying the Journeymen or finding Adalia. She was sure one or the other would happen here, but which one?

"Are you guys getting off at Redemption?" Bounce asked each passenger.

"Why?" Yspeida scowled at him.

"You're the last two. If you two are getting off here as well, I think Gryphilix might cancel the rest of the leg."

"We are going to be staying." Knock weakly answered the question before Yspeida could say anything. Yspeida turned and looked at her. "It might be my last stop in this life, and it might as well be here."

"You aren't going to die," Yspeida scolded her. "I won't allow it."

Knock took on a motherly tone as she spoke. "If I do die, it won't be because my friends didn't help me. It will be because it is my time. Horrible things happen. They even happen to good people. Fate seems cruel at times, but that's just our bias—Fate doesn't care enough to be cruel."

Yspeida collapsed to her knees onto the floor of the coach next to Knock. All of her fellow travelers had become like a family to her, and she didn't want to lose them like she had lost her family to those vicious murderers, the Journeymen. "I..." All her words left her as she was filled up with emotion.

"Cry for them. Cry for all of them." Knock put her hand on Yspeida's knee. "It doesn't mean you're weak. It means you love them. Like brothers and sisters. There is no shame in that."

Yspeida embraced Knock with a tender and gentle hug. "I didn't cry at the funeral pyre of my own family. Why do I cry now?"

"Because you didn't do it then."

"I don't understand." The tears ran down to the armor she wore, and the wetness of the tears stained the leather.

"If you ignore your emotions, they build up," Knock told her. "And once the release comes, it comes like a flood, uncontrollable and much more damaging. Little outpourings stop the damage from building up. And if you don't feel the negative, you'll never enjoy the positive. Day is only day because there is night. Without night, even the day becomes oppressive."

They sat in silence for a while, Yspeida next to Knock. Yspeida could feel that Knock's body was warm, much warmer than it should be. She was feverish and getting worse. Redemption couldn't come soon enough.

"Night for you isn't for a while, Knock. Rest now, and I know we will soon find Dar and get you treated."

"He," Knock whispered as she closed her eyes, "will find us."

Dar was well past halfway down the stairs when he heard somebody coming from farther below. Winter was already out, and he was ready for the attack. He stopped short of the landing and waited so that whatever was coming would be clear of the corner and clear to attack. He put his free hand out and stopped Drij. If it was the daemons, he wanted to give Drij a clear shot to get away.

"Hello?"

It was Adalia.

Dar put his sword down. Drij lurched forward, but Dar put his hand up again, telling him to wait for a moment.

Adalia came around the corner and walked passively to Dar. She didn't reach for him. "It's good to see you. Please get me out of here." Adalia didn't look at Dar when she spoke to him.

"Are you ill? Did they mistreat you?" He tried to look her in the eye, but she had a distant sense to her and didn't return his gaze.

Even Drij noticed. "Is she okay?"

"I think so." Dar frowned.

"Why did you stop me?" Drij stood behind him at a little distance.

"We are dealing with an illusionist. An assassin illusionist. I wanted to make sure it wasn't a trap."

Adalia jumped in. "This is not a trap. The trap is elsewhere."

Both Drij and Dar looked at each other.

Dar spoke first. "Where are we supposed to go?"

"The Lake of Tears."

"Why?"

"We must take May there."

"And is that a trap?" Drij inquired..

"It is not a trap."

Drij took a stab at the questioning. "Why must we take May there?"

"It is not a trap," she repeated.

"It's a shame," Drij said to Dar, "that you don't have enough magic power for a Dispel Magic spell. She's looks to me like she's in some sort of magic trance."

"So I noticed." Dar brought his right hand to his chin, supporting his elbow with his left arm. "I wonder how we can turn this into an advantage."

"With her being this flat, you know, he must have known we would figure it out." Drij leaned against the wall.

"That's the hard part."

Drij said what Dar was thinking. "Walking into the trap or just leaving it alone."

"It is not a trap." Adalia's voice came out in monotone again.

Drij had had enough. "So what is it, then?"

Adalia just looked forward, and the dull, glassy look in her eyes seemed to spread across her face. "The beginning of the new age of the Master."

Both Dar and Drij looked at her.

"Something she must have overheard." Drij pushed off from the wall, ready to move.

Dar nodded. "Time to ambush the trap."

Vulia and Letin stood at the rocky shore of the nearby Lake of Tears. It was a flawless lake. A perfect circle, its surface was smooth as any mirror, and it made the images it reflected brighter somehow. The water was so pure one could see the bottom of the lake some distance down even with the sun being low in the sky. There were no waves, and nothing grew or swam along the small rocks that covered the bottom. Bathing in the water was forbidden, but blessed containers could be dipped in the water. People anointed the dead with the water of the Lake of Tears, believing it guaranteed admission into the Heavens. It was also a supposed to be a proof against the foul beasts from the Hells, since the water from the lake was rumored to be the purest substance in all of Holimoren. Purity that their evil could not corrupt.

Being this close to it made Letin feel sick. Vulia seemed oblivious to the location; he knew she was concerned only about the vessel and conducting the ceremony to bring the Master back to the land of the living.

"Where are they?" she said, not even looking at Letin.

"They could only be here by now if they flew." Letin wondered to himself what would happen if he urinated in the lake.

Out of the corner of his eye, he saw her shoot him a quick glance. "I've seen that look before. Don't even think of defiling the lake. We need it pure for our purpose."

"I wouldn't dream of it," he said, a touch of laughter in his tone. He turned and looked at her. She still wasn't looking at him; instead, her attention was focused in the direction of the town.

"Is this humorous? Have you forgotten our purpose?" she asked.

"We want the same thing but for different reasons." He paused. "We could see if the damage your foot gave me is permanent, if you want to kill some time..."

"Letin." She shook her head and then turned to face him. His pants were already down around his ankles. She started to walk toward him. He was still red and bruised from the kick she'd given him—he knew she could see it. She smiled, and when she was close enough, she did a scissor kick and hit him in the same spot she had damaged earlier. He fell over and was only just able to get out a groan. She ignored him, pulling out a dagger and holding it to his throat.

"That time has passed," she said through gritted teeth. "Never do that again, unless you want to be a gelding."

"But aren't we going to make a vessel for the Master together?" He was crying, and the dagger felt like the least of his worries.

"This is going to succeed, and then I will have the Master's child once he has transformed the vessel into his own flesh.

I don't want your seed in me when the Master is so close at hand. I will not defile the womb of his child any further."

"I am sorry you feel that way."

"At least you know how I feel." She pulled the dagger away from his throat. "Physically and mentally."

"I won't do it again." He pulled his pants up as he stood.

"I see you without clothes again, I will cut you. Understand?"

"Yes." Letin finished straightening his wardrobe.

"Now let's get our spells straight for tomorrow. The dusk is building, and I don't think they will be stupid enough to attack at night."

"I agree." Letin went to take a step but winced and stopped. "I'm going to need more time."

She threw a potion at him, hitting him in the head. "Take that, and let's get ready." She took in a deep breath to settle herself and looked around the area. Trees and boulders of various sizes were scattered around in odd locations across the otherwise open lakeshore. The tallest tree was just maybe the height of single story house, but its trunk was almost two men around. She looked for boulders large enough to help shield them, and found more than a couple. Knowing immediately what would provide cover would be an advantage for them over their enemies.

Dar, Adalia, and Drij walked through the heavy doors of the church and set off down the street. Dar was leading the way, intent on finding something or someone in particular. They proceeded through town in silence, soon enough getting to one of the Wards, which they followed for a bit. Drij watched, following them from a couple of steps back, but he couldn't figure out what Dar was looking for.

Just as Drij was going to ask what Dar was doing, Dar stopped to look at an odd-shaped rock in the low stone wall. The rock was black, which was very different from the tan and gray of the other rocks of the Ward and the even, flat gray of the road. Dar reached out and pushed the rock down, and it sank a couple of inches, farther than Drij would have expected.

"And what are we doing?" Drij asked with a slight hint of mockery in his voice.

"We are looking for an old friend," Dar answered, the same hint of disdain ringing in his words.

"Old like my age, or old like the age of rocks?" Drij smiled.

"Funny. His name is Gliindr."

"The dwarven digger fellow?" Drij came over and looked at the rock.

"The very same." Dar stood back and motioned Drij to keep back.

After about five seconds, the rock popped back into place and made a clicking noise. There was brief pause, and then the ground to either side of the wall around the stone, about one foot in diameter, began to rise into the air. It was a hatch, and as the waning daylight flooded into the hole, they saw three dwarves, each with a pick ax in his hand and a hammer at his belt. They were standing on a ladder made of iron, and they did not appear to be happy.

"What be you wanting?" called out the first one.

"Gliindr. I wish to speak to him that controls the tunnels." Dar kneeled so as to not loom over the trio.

"What be your reason?" The second one spoke this time.

"I have a job for him." Dar pulled out a coin purse and held it by its strings.

"How much you be paying?" said the third.

"A hundred." Dar looked the first dwarf in the eye. "Plus a bonus per man that helps."

"He's down below." The second dwarf pulled on the leg of the first, who stood a few rungs above him on the ladder. "Why don't you come back at dawn."

Dar was just about nose to nose with the first. "Why don't you let us in now, and we'll have you paid by dawn."

The third started heading down the ladder. "That will cost extra."

"So be it." Dar motioned for the first dwarf to make room for him on the ladder.

Drij turned to Adalia. "Prepare to climb a ladder, dear girl."

She spoke for the first time in a while. "Are we heading to the Lake of Tears?"

Dar yelled from down below, "Yes. Now get down here!"

She climbed down the ladder, and Drij followed suit. When they were all below ground, the hatch came down and locked into position.

Gryphilix was yawning again when Yspeida made her way up front to where he sat, holding the reins. "How much longer until we stop for the night?" she asked. "How far until Redemption?"

Gryphilix turned and looked at her. She had been crying again. The halfling must not be doing better yet. "Tonight we stop next to the Lake of Tears, then we hit Redemption in the morning. Radby doesn't like late-night visitors. It wakes him up."

"Radby?" She looked off into the distance. Gone were the thick forests of the shoulders of the Skyneedle, replaced with scrub bushes, hardtack ground, and the occasional stand of willows.

"The Lord Mayor of Redemption. Nice, pompous, rules with an iron hand in a white linen glove. Good enough fellow, I suppose. But if we show up after dusk, he'll never let me into town again. I get enough travelers who drop dead before they arrive already—I don't need to make them walk the Wards."

She nodded and went to head back to her spot.

"If it makes it any easier, lass, there are no evil ones near the Lake of Tears. It makes them sick. At least the stupid ones."

"Is what they say about the lake true?" She walked back up to the front of the coach.

"What do they say about the lake?" Gryphilix shot her a glance then focused again on the road.

"That it can cure everything and anything." There was a slight hint of hope in her voice.

"I never heard of anybody getting healed by the lake itself, but I know some charlatans sell water from nearby streams— the fools hope it will help them to their destiny."

"So the Lake of Tears does nothing?" Defeat was creeping back into her voice.

"I didn't say that." Gryphilix concentrated on the road ahead. "I just said I never heard of its healing people. But that doesn't rule out a miracle."

"Gliindr!" Dar reached out and grabbed the forearm of the burly fellow, who grabbed his forearm at the same time.

"Long time no see, Dar of the Silver."

Drij chuckled at Dar's new title. "Hello."

"A shield carrier?" Gliindr eyed up Drij, and by his expression he found him wanting.

"A business associate."

Gliindr turned his attention to the fair Adalia. "A seed carrier?" The rest of Gliindr's digging team laughed at his ribald joke.

"Another business associate." Dar tried not to look offended at the crude nature of his friend.

Drij, however, appeared taken aback. "She's trying to get her dead daughter to Redemption. I believe a little respect is in order."

"Redemption is a lovely town." Gliindr coldly eyed Drij. "But it ain't no place of forgiveness."

All the dwarves started in at once. "Work is the only salvation!"

Drij looked around the lot of them. Dar watched as he sized them up—each was about four feet tall, with a long flowing beard and bright brown eyes. Some were missing teeth, others missing fingers, but none were missing a mischievous spirit.

"My name is Gliindr, newcomer."

"Drij."

"I nary meant any offense to your gentle sensibilities. You see, we don't get many women down here."

"And thems that do have beards!" shouted one of the crew.

Dar waited for the laughter to stop before he made his proposition. "I need to get the three of us to within two hundred paces of the Lake of Tears without being seen."

"And you figured old Gliindr would get you there underground." Gliindr pulled out a pipe and stuck it in this mouth. It was a short pipe and didn't appear to have been smoked in some time. "What's the matter, you walking into a trap?"

Adalia spouted her new favorite thing to say: "It is not a trap."

Gliindr looked at her like she wasn't real. Then he shook his head. "What you're proposing will cost you. I don't let surface folk down here. This is the earth of the dwarves, and we work it fair."

"Aren't these tunnels actually illegal?" As Drij spoke, Dar winced. "If the Lord Mayor finds out, or some of those that believe you're committing sacrilege, you could end up out of business."

Gliindr narrowed his eyes before easing up and letting a bit of smirk out. "We could end up dead, actually. That's a bit more permanent than 'out of business.' I can handle out of business." He winked at one of the dwarves nearby. "Been that way a couple of times. But dead is something I'd rather wait on."

"He said he'd pay a hundred plus," spouted one of the crew, one of the ladder gang.

Dar knew the heart of the dwarves. Precious metals and gems were required to get them on your side, or to get them motivated. "One hundred gold for the crew, plus a platinum coin per man who works his share."

"Sounds like even money to me." Gliindr spat in his palm and held it out for Dar to shake. Dar spat in his hand and shook it with vigor. "When do we start?"

"We need to be there just after dawn."

Gliindr squinted at him. "How many dawns from now?"

"One. I want to be there tomorrow."

All the dwarves looked like they had just sucked on a sour fruit. Gliindr looked at them and rubbed his hands.

"I should have asked that first." Then he turned and yelled loud enough to be heard by all, "Step lively, boys, we got a lot of work to do!"

Dar and Drij took Adalia to a quiet section of the tunnel system, one close to where the dwarves were expanding their labyrinth of access ways and conduits. Dar pulled a wineskin containing a potion from his pack and told Adalia to have good drink from it. She nodded and did as she was commanded. She pulled the wineskin away from her lips and promptly passed out, with Dar catching her before she could hit the ground. Then, to be safe, he wrapped rope around her feet so she wouldn't be able to wander away. Then he set up a makeshift camp and laid out his bedroll. He started to meditate and focus on his spells. Tomorrow would be quite a day, he imagined. He needed to be ready.

"Dar?" Drij was meditating next to Dar. Well, he had been meditating.

Dar didn't open his eyes. "Yes?"

"Before we fight tomorrow, I think you should know what happened to me."

"If you feel you're ready, I'm ready to listen."

Unlike the way Drij had told some of his other stories, there was no urgency to his tone. A tinge of sorrow maybe, but right away it sounded to Dar that Drij had been thinking about this a lot. "I used to be a powerful cleric. I followed the ways of the old gods, which I know now are the True Gods. I had it all: nice family, loving wife, three wonderful kids, a perfect house, and a growing following in the church. I was the town pastor, and this wasn't a small town. I could have been Lord Mayor—I could have become the regional head of the church."

"But you got bored." Dar changed positions but otherwise remained in his meditative pose. In his experience, people were often more talkative when they weren't being watched.

"Listless, unexcited; yes, I would have to say bored. It all came so easily. I was not challenged. So I took a journey of faith. While on this journey, a dream came to me. I was near the Forest of Shade near Eagles Glen. A haunting place, full of dark shadows and brilliant hues. I figured I would find adventure or at least some evil there to fight. How ironic now, in hindsight—I did find evil there that day, but I didn't fight it. I lost myself to it."

"In what way?" Dar used a gentle tone.

Drij took a deep breath before continuing. "Thinking back on it now, I believe I was visited by an evil presence, but I took its words as the truth instead of the slander and libel that it really was. That was the day I turned away from being just and fair and became full of rage and evil..." Drij's voice drifted off, and he sounded lost in thought.

Drij walked around the shadowy forest, his walking staff in hand. The knapsack full of odds and ends that made life easier weighed him down little, but it was getting late, so he put the pack down on the ground. He set up a small ring of stones to build a fire pit, but oddly enough, the stones were already warm. Once the fire was burning, he reached into the pack and took out some iron rations. Seemingly named for their texture, they were hard to chew unless soaked in water, though most adventurers used beer or some other type of alcohol. Drij had no brew with him, so the water would have to do. The water tasted earthy, and his thoughts drifted back to where he had gotten the water, from the stream near his house. He munched in silence as the smoke from the fire started to billow. Drij watched as the cloud slowly took form—oddly, it didn't seem affected by the light but occasional breeze that always seemed to flutter through the forest.

For the entire time it took him to eat the ration, he watched. More and more, it started to look like a person. He could see a head—without features, of course—and then a torso and maybe hair and a long, gaunt neck. Arms and legs were also visible, but he figured the fading light must be playing tricks on him.

"Time to leave, smoke man."

"Why?" came the hollow-sounding reply.

Drij flew to his feet and grabbed his staff. He spun around and looked for the source of the voice.

"I'm right here, Drij." The words echoed off of the trees.

"Who are you?"

"That is of no importance. I come from another place, another time, and it is hard for me to remain, even in this dark place, in this form."

Drij turned and looked at the shadowy form the smoke had finished creating on the other side of the fire. It was clearly a man, tall and thin, but all other features were faded out by the smoke and the flickering light from the fire.

"You are the greatest cleric in your family, in your town, in your region," it said. "But you don't get the respect you deserve. You must make them respect you."

"You can't make people respect you." Drij tightened the grip on his staff.

"You can't make them love you either. But you can make them fear you. People respect fear. They respect being commanded. They need a firm hand. There is a book called the Book of Truth. Seek it. Once you have found it, learn its every page. It will be your guide to a new age in Holimoren. You will be the first of my order in your part of the land, and rewards will come to you."

"Are you a messenger from the gods?"

The shadow man laughed. "You might say that. I am a messenger." A tendril of smoke came out of the arm of the smoky figure and headed toward Drij. He took a whiff of it, and it snaked up his nose like a tentacle. Drij blinked and struggled and fell to the ground.

"And you," said the slowly disappearing shadow man, "will be my message."

"I wandered for a time after that," Drij said, "and I quickly found a new church, the Order of the Holy. There they talked about the Book of Truth, and I understood my new role. I was to spread the word. The book preached how sacrifice, hard work, and faithfulness were not the way to true enlightenment but rather the signs of a lazy mind and a weak soul. I watched and later participated in massive orgies disguised as holy rituals, counted the coins as the Holy churches got fat off of the contributions of the towns they grew into, and helped them to bilk the locals out of hard-earned monies. Each town always had evil befall it before the church arrived, and then the evil would disappear after the church was founded."

"The church was founded by those who were doing the evil?"

Drij paused a moment, perhaps nodding—Dar still had not opened his eyes. "So they could seem like saviors. They were both the cause and the cure—no wonder each town fell under their sway. I enjoyed being the savior; I enjoyed the excitement of chasing the evil—and the women. I was so busy becoming what the book described that I never took a look at what the outcome was going to be. I had gone against everything in my original vows to my gods, my wife, and to myself. So I went walking again, and I ran into the Second. He pulled me into a sweat lodge, and soon the smoke was billowing out of the flames. The wood was probably from the Forest of Shadows, and it was just like being with the shadow-and-smoke man. Again I got dizzy, and I passed out, straight into the fire."

"How did you survive that?" Dar shifted his legs, trying to keep as quiet as possible.

"I had cast Return before I left home on my original journey, and it activated when I passed out from smoke inhalation and fell into the fire. I woke up in the foyer of my home. It was late at night, but I knew the layout perfectly. I walked into the kitchen, pulled out a butchering knife, and went around to my sleeping family, killing each one in turn. It was like I was watching somebody else do these acts of unspeakable evil. I kept stabbing, and the blood kept flying. I started to write something with the blood on one wall, but my wife had a friend of mine cast an Invisible Stalker spell while I was gone. The creature raced from room to room, always trailing behind me in my bloody spree, until at last it caught up with me. And when it did, the creature seized me, wrestled me down, and held me until the gardener found me the next morning."

Dar opened his eyes. Drij was crying now, and tears were falling down onto his lap.

"My wife had set the assistant to only capture, not kill. But its anger was fierce. The Guard had to cast Dispel Magic to get the being to release me. And as soon as I was released, they put me into chains. I was taken to court, and they put me on trial. I was a different man—combative, hostile, and so profane that they had to put a gag on me. It struck the Father from my old church that I wasn't normal, and I needed to be cleansed. They cast Dispel Evil to make sure I wasn't still under the effects of some demon possession or magic jar. At that point, smoke tendrils came out of my body and fled up the chimney."

Drij dabbed his nose with his sleeve and continued with his tale.

"I remained in custody, but because I'd been under the influence of that thing, they couldn't prosecute me beyond eviction. The leaders of the town cast me out of the town forever, never to return. The sister of my beloved dead wife started a campaign to see justice done, though, and I was declared a criminal in most of the towns around the Highstar plains. So I fled to Holin. But my sister-in-law's bounty hunters preceded me."

"Where you hired me to help you come here to die."

Drij's expression shifted from remorse to thoughtfulness. "But now I believe that the shadow man was Letin or Vulia casting a spell on me. They made me evil. And they did it for their master."

"Kygger. That is why you went so silent while at Mrix's castle."

Drij nodded. "It all fell into place."

"And now?" Dar laid down, ready for bed. Drij did the same.

Drij sighed. "Now I will confront Vulia and Letin and make them pay for their sins against me and my family." Dar had just about drifted off to sleep when Drij finished his thought. "Or die trying."

In the Ethereal plane, the shadowy figure drifted forward in the resistanceless infinity that was his current home. As he glanced around, the hazy outline of the real world was everywhere he looked. In this state he could walk through walls, travel underground, and keep an eye on all of his various plans. He had already checked on the first team. They were fighting too much; it was something he hadn't foreseen. But this part of the plan was working nicely. The woman would betray them all, and he would join the baby. Or he would wait for the closet, now that he knew where it was. Only when a body crossed the dimensions would he have his chance, and here were two in one place at one time. And if this didn't work, he had more time. He had all the time in this world—and the next.

But for his next attempt, he wouldn't pick a brother and sister to orchestrate his return.

TWELVE

Fate

Rarely is the climactic battle known to be such
beforehand. Usually, it's a small skirmish that gets
out of hand and becomes the grand ending.
—Elader the Old

Dar assumed it was dawn, as the dwarves were all standing over him, looking at each other, trying to figure out
which should wake him.

"You do it."

"You do it," came a baritone voice.

"Gentlemen, it is already done." Dar ended the debate by
sitting up.

"We just haves to punch the final hole up to the surface,
and you're ready to go, Mr. Dar, sir." Gliindr stationed himself
between the two debating dwarves and looked down at Dar in
his bedroll. Their leader still had his miner's lantern on, but it
appeared to have gone out awhile ago.

"Perfect," Dar said. "Uncover anything…interesting?"

"Well, there was that vein of pl..." started one of the smaller dwarves. Each of his fellows turned toward him, and he never finished the sentence.

"Not a thing," claimed Gliindr, whose face was overwhelmed by a smile.

"I imagine you want payment, then?" Dar looked over at Drij, who was putting away his bedroll. Drij turned and handed a small bag to Dar.

"That's all I've got," Drij said to Dar. Dar noted that Drij looked refreshed for the first time since they had met.

Dar reached into his belt and pulled out a large number of platinum and gold coins, which he placed into the small sack. He tossed it Gliindr. "I believe that will settle things."

Gliindr took the sack and made the coins inside jingle. Then he let it hang. He considered its weight for moment.

"One hundred and fiftyish gold coins, and about forty platinum."

"Sounded like a couple silver in there too, Gliindr," said the smaller fellow.

Gliindr looked at Dar. "We are settled." He smiled.

"We'll collect our female friend and be off then." Dar motioned to Drij to get Adalia.

"She's not here," Drij said, a touch of panic in his voice.

"Not here?" Dar turned toward Gliindr. "Any idea where our friend went off to?"

"I don't have any clue." Gliindr was looking sour. But behind him the smaller fellow was bouncing his head up and down.

"I suppose you know, don't you, friend?" Dar went over the fellow. Dar dropped to one knee so he wasn't looming over the barely three-and-half-foot-tall dwarf.

"She wandered past me about twenty minutes ago. She was heading to the opening just before the new one we had to dig to meet the deal." He smiled, happy to have helped out.

Dar cut that smile short. "Did you not think to stop her?"

"Stop a customer? No, sir, never crossed my mind." The short fellow beamed ear to ear again. "I did help her out of that rope around her legs. It was slowing her down something fierce."

Gliindr rubbed his eyes with his right hand. "Sorry, sir, but we didn't know."

Dar waved his hand. "It matters not. They knew we were coming anyway."

They stood in silence for a moment, both Dar and Drij, it seemed, waiting for Adalia to say it wasn't a trap.

Drij broke the silence. "But it *is* a trap."

Dar and Drij walked off toward the opening, with Gliindr leading the way. The other dwarves remained behind.

"Which is more crazy, the fact that they head to their death, or that they joke about it?" echoed through the tunnels and caught up to Dar and Drij. They ignored it and pressed on.

"Gwilli, open up the good stuff, and we'll toast to their funeral!"

Letin and Vulia sat on the low boulder near an old trail that led up to the lake, and Adalia rest uncomfortably between them. Set askew, the shape of their seating arrangement allowed better sight lines. Letin watched the hostage, hoping she would come over to him. Vulia was sharpening a long sword, her visage marked by stern forbearance. Letin knew she made that scowl when she was trying to remember her favorite spells.

"Are you ready, Letin?" She kept the whetstone working against the face of the blade. "Does the girl's arrival alone mean things are already unraveling?"

"I don't need a lot of time to be ready. I need to keep loose." He fought off the impulse to look at his sister. "The plan is still fine."

"What is the plan?"

"For her to come to me. I mean, them."

"She isn't going to come to you." She shot him daggers with her eyes.

"I know." He was still sore anyway.

"Then why are you looking at her that way?"

"I enjoy looking at pretty things." He held his gaze on Adalia. "Especially pretty ones that won't kill me."

Vulia rolled her eyes and flipped the sword over.

"I doubt you'll need that sword," he said. "My magic will defeat them. I'll hit them with all of my most destructive spells: Magic Missiles, Disintegration, Fireball, Lightning Bolt, and my favorite, Reverse Gravity. They'll fall to their death when it runs out."

"I'll keep plan B ready just in case." She held out the sword.

"Your time, I guess." He stopped himself from suggesting anything further. That sword would geld him quick.

Vulia finished sharpening the sword, rubbed it with oil on it to stop any corrosion, and put it back into the slender leather sleeve that shielded it from the elements. She leaned to the left and stretched to the right, making sure all her muscles were loose for the upcoming battle. "You're sure you don't want to make a better plan, Letin?"

"Yes, Vulia." He frowned at her. "I know what I'm doing."

"But *I* don't know what you are doing."

It was Letin's turn to roll his eyes. "You stay back, I bombard them back to the beginning of time, and they meet their makers. Then we take the Closet of Xio and get the vessel for Master."

"Won't all of your heavy-duty spells like Disintegrate damage the closet?"

Letin's look of confidence evaporated, and he looked at the ground in complete disbelief.

"I'll take that as a yes."

"But…I…but…"

"Time for a new plan?"

Letin just stared off into the early-morning sky, checking off a list of spells that were not going to be effective in the upcoming battle. "If I use some spells like Fireball as an air burst, the flames will damage the others but won't hurt the one with the closet. It will take some fine skills, but I know I can do it." Letin stood before continuing. "That's it! I can use the spells in an auxiliary role and support you in beheading the fool."

"Remember," she told him, "after this, I go alone. Brother or not, our partnership is through."

Letin didn't hear her—he was already thinking out what his first words to his master would be.

Adalia adjusted her position and sat straight on the hard-packed pebbles. Neither sibling noticed her rubbing her eyes and then suddenly snapping back to her original position, eyes darting around the scene.

Dar and Drij were now at the mouth of the opening that Gliindr had dug for them. The crew had given it an impromptu hatch, with a ladder leading up to the surface. Gliindr had let them walk the last hundred yards on their own, as it was all fresh dig and there weren't any other passageways, so there was no other way out. Dar paused at the base of the ladder.

Dar looked at Drij, who was holding a war hammer. "When we…" He stopped and pointed at the new weapon. "Where did you get that?"

"One of the dwarves gave it to me. She said I was doing something very brave and it would be good if I could defend myself."

"She?" Dar shook his head. "Never mind, here is the plan." Dar caught Drij's eye to make sure he was listening. "We'll stay close together. You get Adalia and go back underground. Their magic will have less effect underground."

"That's not true," Drij countered. "It will be just as effective, and the narrow tunnels will focus area-of-effect spells."

Dar grimaced at being caught. "Okay, I simplified too much, but the narrow area makes it too risky for them to try much. A lightning bolt in a tunnel like this will bounce back at you, and then you're fried."

"What about Letin and Vulia?" Drij tried swinging the hammer, apparently in an effort to gauge how best to use it.

"If you get a shot, take it. They are part of the problem, but this is about Adalia. As long as she is with them, she is in danger. Once she is safe, we can come back and get them."

"What about a parley? If they talk, will we listen?"

"Violence is never my first choice. But it is the favorite choice of evil. At least in my experience." Dar looked him in the eye. "As long as they have Adalia, we have no leverage."

"Right." Drij directed his head in a slow circle. "I stretch my neck when I'm nervous."

Dar pressed on. "On three. Ready?"

"Ready."

Dar put his leg on the bottom rung.

"Three!"

As soon as Dar broached the surface, he was sure that at least Vulia could see them coming out of the ground beside the lake. The evil pair was standing between him and Drij and the town, with Adalia apparently safe between them. But that also meant that Drij and Dar were between all of them and the lake. Each blocked the other's escape route. But they were dangerously close, maybe ten yards away from one another.

"Letin," Vulia said, "behind you."

Dar met the stare of the gaunt magic user as the wizard turned to face them. "Give us the girl, and we'll be on our way."

Letin curled his fingers and clenched his fist, appearing to be working out the kinks in his hand. "Give us the baby, and we'll be on our way to meet our destiny."

"You know we can't do that. That baby belongs to her mother."

Letin looked at Vulia. "Is that not a delicious turn of fate? A little girl? The Master won't be happy, having to live in the body of a little girl, but I bet he won't mind." He smiled a wicked grin. "Makes you being queen a bit harder, though."

"Focus, Letin." Vulia gritted her teeth, and the venom of her tone was clear.

"You should know that I have trapped her," Letin told Dar, rolling up his sleeves. "If she leaves my sight, she dies."

"A bluff," whispered Drij. He looked at Letin, appearing to be staring into his soul. "Nothing more, nothing less."

Dar stood there motionless. His eyes were on Letin but quickly darted to Adalia. She appeared to be nodding very slowly, looking at Drij. Dar quickly turned his head so Vulia and Letin couldn't see his eyes. He didn't want to give away what he'd glimpsed.

"Then we had better not do anything," he said to Drij.

Dar pulled out the Dagger of the Wasps and flung it at Letin's head. Letin finished his first spell just as the dagger flew into the protected area of its magical aura. The dagger hit an invisible shield and crashed to the ground. The handle of the dagger turned into wings and it flew back toward Dar, directing itself back into the scabbard he had drawn it from.

Drij started his own spell and created a wall of stone from that rose from the earth. He ran behind it, and Dar moved to get on the safe side of the stone haven as well. He had just made it as a dagger from Vulia smashed into the edge of its granite surface, ricocheting away to end up on the ground slightly behind the wall. Drij noticed a black liquid flow from inside the dagger.

"Poison!" Drij barked. He focused inward for moment before abandoning the effort. "I can't recall my Cure Poison spell. We need a plan to protect ourselves."

Dar pulled out Weeper and prepared to fire. "I have a curative potion. If you get hit, let me know and I'll give it to you."

"Right." Drij peeked around the corner. "Adalia is alone, about fifty feet from us and forty feet from them."

"Time to let Weeper do her work. When I get them down, go get her." Dar turned and let fly an arrow from his unending supply. The arrow flew across the area and struck the invisible shield. He aimed his next round at Vulia, and she dodged behind the tree just in time. The arrow flew past her head and impacted the tree behind them.

Letin had picked his next spell. Dar recognized the opening of the spell and leaned back behind the rock wall.

"Fireball!"

Drij leaned back as well, but to their surprise, the ball wasn't aimed at the face of the rock. It exploded above the wall, and the ball of flame expanded about ten feet above the ground. Letin had misjudged the distance this one time. But the fireball had filled the sky above the battle, creating an impressive show.

Yspeida was waiting for the coach wagon to get going for the morning when she saw a massive ball of red and orange off in the distance. It expanded into the sky in a perfect sphere just about a half mile away before disappearing.

She had to investigate. She took off running in the direction of the flames.

Behind her by a dozen strides already, Bounce took off after her.

And Knock watched it all, pale and weak.

After the fireball, both sides took a moment to regain their composure and contemplate their next move. Drij was happy to remain under the relative safety and cover of the stone wall, and Dar didn't seem to be in a rush either. Dar snapped his fingers and got Drij's attention. He pointed at Drij and then turned an imaginary corner with his fingers. Then he pointed at himself and held up his hand in a way that indicated a stop and then repeated the turning-a-corner motion. Drij nodded. Dar finished the discussion by holding up all ten fingers. Drij nodded again, and both turned to face their ends of the wall. Each counted to ten, with Drij being just a little bit faster.

He turned to look out into the field of fire only to be tackled and run over by Adalia. She continued as soon as she could and scrambled to the center of wall. Drij rolled back behind the wall, the wind knocked out of him.

Dar, already committed to turning the corner, Weeper at the ready, only let one arrow fly before returning to the start position. He turned and leaned against the wall, visually inspecting Drij, who finally caught his breath. Dar turned his attention to Adalia, who was still winded from her sprint—and, it seemed, just a touch hysterical.

"Are you wounded?"

Adalia's eye met Dar's, and she rushed forward to take Dar into an embrace. But her movement was too sudden for Dar to adjust to the extra weight and they both fell over, with Adalia on top of him. She nestled into his chest and sobbed.

Drij decided to give the two their moment, so he walked over to the end of the wall and peered around the corner. He scanned left and right but couldn't pick out where either of their foes were located. He heard a sound off to the left of where he had last seen Letin, but he figured it was a spell—though even as a master of the clerical arts, he didn't recognize it. Drij leaned back and waited for the spell to resolve itself.

He did not have to wait long.

The wall was gone, except for the lowest three inches that ran along the soil.

Dar immediately knew what had happened. "Disintegration! Scramble for cover!"

Dar helped Adalia to her feet and took off for the nearby cluster of trees. Drij, being closer to a boulder, ran for it. They were now separated by almost twenty feet, with Letin still some forty feet away from each of them.

Dar looked out and saw very little—he had a good idea where Letin was, but not knowing where Vulia was made him worry. Letin's shield was still out where the wall used to be, and without a target, Weeper was useless. He felt the closeness of Adalia and drank in her warmth for a moment before coming to decision. He had to get her out of the battle. He turned to look at her and break the news when, out of the corner of his eye, he noticed Yspeida coming into sight at a full run.

"Take cover!" It was Drij who got the warning out first.

She stopped and hid behind the nearest tree. She peered out and looked for the enemy. Not finding any, she focused on Dar.

"How many?" she called out—wisely, without exposing herself to the fire of the enemy.

"Two," Dar yelled.

"What are their abilities?"

"A magic user and an assassin." Drij, being less experienced in combat, exposed himself to the enemy position and was narrowly missed by a small crossbow bolt. It stuck the tree he was leaning against. Even from where Dar crouched, he could smell the pungent poison on the small bolt. The bolt wound by itself wouldn't have been fatal, but the poison appeared to be potent.

"Assemble at Yspeida," Dar called out. He cast a spell, and dense fog descended on the battle arena. He took Adalia's hand and took off running for Yspeida's cover position. Drij arrived a moment later.

"We need to settle the score here." Dar looked at each of them, trying to see how they were dealing with the battle. Drij nodded when Dar met his eye. "I need you to take Adalia out of the battle. She is—"

Yspeida jumped in. "An untrained noncombatant in a war zone and thus a liability. I agree. She needs to be removed to safety."

Dar nodded. "And I want you, Drij, to do it."

Drij was about to say something when Dar stopped him. "Yspeida and I are trained for this. We know how to fight, and if things go bad, I'll get us out of here." He handed the Closet of Xio to Drij. "This must not get into their hands."

Drij swallowed hard, his eyes wide. "How will we get out of here?"

Dar paused for a second. "Take the tunnels. We are about thirty feet from the opening, and this fog will give you cover. I'll go with you, since that will put me on their flank." He looked at Yspeida. "Once they figure out this is a magical fog, Letin will cast Dispel Magic and remove it. I'll be over there"—he pointed toward the point where they had come out of the ground—"and they should come to me. You circle behind them and attack from that angle. They are both very powerful, so be watchful."

Yspeida nodded.

Dar ended the meeting by saying, "Let's go."

Letin was scanning the fog when Vulia came up and touched him on the shoulder. He turned his head a little to hear her whispers.

"I don't think this is a normal fog, Letin."

"Why is that, dear sister?" He didn't stop his scanning. "The fact that thick fog just appeared from nowhere was your clue?"

"Plus it ends just about thirty feet behind us." Vulia held up her crossbow. "Why didn't you get rid of it right away?"

"I was saving my magic for the most powerful spells."

"Which you can't use if you can't see them. Get rid of it."

"Right." Letin stood and started the long spell that would allow him to cancel other magicks. As soon as it was over, the fog disappeared, revealing the ranger off in the distance, picking up his shield. The cleric and the woman were nowhere to be seen, and for a moment Letin got mad. His plan wasn't faring very well. This battle was supposed to be over.

"Guard my back. I'll Fireball him again."

He went through the physical motions and the magic phrases quickly, and a streak of fire leaped from his hand and flew over to the area where ranger was at and exploded in a sphere of flames. After the flames cleared, Letin looked out, expecting to see the charred body of his foe. But what he saw infuriated him. The target had hid behind a shield and was still alive.

"No shield could withstand that blast," Letin said in disgust.

Vulia squinted at the shield. "It's covered in red dragon scales. It's fireproof."

"Really?" Letin looked at it intently. "Interesting usage of the scales. I'll give it to you as a present once we kill him."

Yspeida had run hard under the cover of the fog to get behind Letin and Vulia but ended up in a gulch that showed signs of being an old river bed. The color of the land was the same as the land around it, so it was very hard to see. Yspeida had fallen into the crease in the ground and was using it for cover. She peeked above the edge and looked for the enemy. She saw them away from where she had gone after them. She had run at an angle from their position in the fog. Dar was now north, the foes to the northeast. She watched as Letin started a spell and the fire flew from his hands and blossomed into a red-and-orange globe of destruction. She was so focused on it that she barely heard Bounce join her in the depression. She turned and looked at him. His face was blank. He nodded at her, and she nodded at him. She turned, located Letin again, and started to figure out a good route to close the distance and end this battle.

She had just picked a route when she felt the sting of pain from a sudden impact to her head, which, a moment later, robbed her of consciousness. Bounce put away his blackjack and surveyed the same route.

Dar peered out from behind his shield. It was his turn for a spell. He uttered the magic phrase and was instantly shifted via the spell Dimension Door to five feet behind Letin. It took Dar a moment to realize he was facing the wrong way—the natural chaos of magic could play tricks at inappropriate times—but he pulled out Winter and corrected his orientation with a spin. He extended the blade, and the arcing weapon forced Letin to duck and dodge. Vulia already had her own weapon drawn and charged into the fray. The clank of steel meeting steel rang throughout the clearing as Vulia's weapon was blocked by Winter. The cold blade radiated its chill into her weapon, and she maneuvered the blade from the clench. She raised her blade again and swung toward Dar's midsection.

Again Dar blocked the blow, and he shifted his weigh, pushing against her. She stepped back, almost failing to keep her balance, and Dar took advantage of that by pressing his attack—only a quick parry saved Vulia from being cut in two. Dar spun out of the move and pointed his sword at the ground in front of him. Letin backed away to give them room and just watched, grinning, seemingly happy to let Vulia do all the work. She charged again, and Dar stepped aside. She placed her pivot foot in the icy patch Winter had just made, lost her footing, and pitched forward. As she fell, she lost her weapon, tumbling to land on her backside with her arms behind her. Letin just laughed.

"You're finished, ranger," he taunted.

Dar had ended up with his back to where Vulia had ended up, but he had heard her weapon come free. He was facing Letin, and nothing was between him and Dar's sword. But still Letin didn't seem to be worried.

"I think it is you who are finished, Letin." Dar took a step forward and raised his sword. The sound of footsteps behind him forced him to pause and turn to assess the new threat.

Bounce was between him and Vulia. He had two swords, one in his left hand and one tucked into his belt next to his normal weapon, a slightly curved dagger. Dar recognized the swords as Yspeida's weapons.

"You're outnumbered, ranger." Letin took another step back, apparently in case Dar made any sudden moves. "He works for us."

Dar looked into Bounce's eyes and found profound sadness. Dar knew that Bounce was not happy to betray him, but betray him he would. Dar got into a defensive position and awaited his fate.

"He has been on our side the whole time." Letin circled around to Vulia and Bounce, never allowing the distance between him and Dar to shorten. "He joined our little group before taking a job with that horrible coach wagon. I'm glad it has paid off."

Vulia rolled her eyes. "Bounce, help me up."

Bounce smiled at her. "Sure thing, lover."

The smile drained from Letin's face. "What do you mean, Bounce?"

Bounce finished bringing Vulia to her feet and looked around, befuddled by the turn in Letin's tone. He looked at Vulia. She appeared to be begging him with her eyes, shaking her head just enough to be seen from Dar's position.

"I don't get it," Bounce said and turned to face Letin.

"You called her 'lover.' What do mean by that?" Letin was about ten feet away from them when Vulia started to back away.

"I mean, you know." Bounce smiled, clearly trying to figure out why this was so wrong. "I did bed your sister, but we have an understanding. We both knew it was just for fun."

Letin took out his dagger and jumped on Bounce. "She belongs to me." He buried the dagger into Bounce's chest again and again and again. The blood covered his clothes.

The moment Letin moved, Dar started running, Winter ready to strike. Vulia pulled out a small item and threw it at the ground. It exploded upon impact, and a thick black smoke covered the area. Dar began to swing blindly, and his fourth stroke, a backhand, caught something off the center of the cutting edge and stopped.

A thump followed, and Dar knew he had connected with something solid. He didn't feel the normal flex of the blade as it cut into something—there was no sliding feel—so he must have hit his target with the flat of the blade. He no longer heard the sickening sounds of Letin's weapon stabbing Bounce. So Dar paused, kneeled, and closed his eyes to protect them from the acrid smoke.

It took almost a minute for the smoke and haze to clear. When it did, Dar rose to his feet, opened his eyes, and looked around. Letin was unconscious, sprawled out on the ground, having apparently been struck in the side of his head. Bounce had suffered at least a dozen stab wounds, and Dar immediately knew there was nothing that could be done for him. Dar leaned over to close the eyes of the dead rogue and shut his mouth. He stood and looked around.

Vulia was gone.

Dar put Winter away and set his shield down. He pulled Letin away from Bounce and looked at his wound. The flat of the blade had hit right above his ear and knocked him out. Dar took the magic user's weapons and bound his hands behind him, being careful to tie each finger to the others. Captive magic users with free fingers were quickly free magic users, in his experience.

Dar was thinking about his next move when Yspeida walked up. She looked at the two men on the ground with no sign of emotion.

"Bounce betrayed me," she said slowly. "Betrayed us."

"I know." Dar looked at the body. "He paid for his sins."

"You killed him?" Yspeida pulled her swords from Bounce's grip and belt. She didn't bother to remove the blood on them.

Dar nodded in Letin's direction. "He did."

"No honor amongst thieves?"

"Evil will turn on itself eventually." Dar studied the lad's face. If not for the blood on it, he might be taken for just sleeping. "I had my doubts about him, but I had no idea he had so fully sided with the forces of evil. I thought maybe he could still chose the straight and narrow."

Yspeida reached out and touch Dar's shoulder. "You did not know. He chose his road, and perhaps the gods will redeem him in time." She turned her attention to Letin. "What of the prisoner?"

Dar had been thinking the same thing. "I really have no idea. I know he's a powerful magic user—and quite mad."

"Isn't he the one who was on the coach wagon?" Yspeida stood over him, looking like she might kick him.

Letin groaned and started to move.

"I think our monster is awake." Dar dropped one knee to the ground and pondered their next course of action.

Yspeida's and Letin's eyes met as he finally shook off the force of the blow that had dropped him. "Where is she?"

Yspeida stood back. "She isn't here. Whoever she is."

"Vulia. She's my sister. Where is she?"

Dar stood. "Your sister? You said she was your lover."

A crooked smile fluttered on Letin's lips. "She was both. And much better at one role than the other."

"You disgust me." Yspeida spit on his robes.

"Can't have that, can I?" Letin sneered at Yspeida. "Ah... the barbarian whore."

Yspeida kicked him in the ribs. Dar just looked on.

"How brave is the wicked she-warrior. Kicking a bound man when he's down." Letin's eyes glared with fire. He sat up and spread his legs to keep his balance, which forced Yspeida to take a step back. "You're lucky you tied me up so well, or I would show you both the true power here."

"What was your plan, Letin?" Dar tried to keep his mind focused on improving the situation.

"Not going to happen." He smiled at Yspeida. "You know, I recognize you."

Yspeida fingered the pommels of Hack and Slash, which she'd just put away. "Really?"

"In the retched Untamed Lands north of the Torrents, you were in the chieftain's hut with a woman who was with child, were you not?"

"How did you know that?"

Letin laughed. "How do I know that?"

"Yspeida, don't let him get to you." Dar got up and started to pace. Brother, sister, lover, wizards in the Untamed Lands, Bounce, it was all too much at once. He needed to think. "He's trying to goad you into releasing him for a fight."

"Yes, honorable warrior. Fight me," Letin said. "You know you want to know the details. You know you want to know why I broke into your family's house. You want to know why I killed your sister or mother or lover or whatever she was. You want to know why I ripped the baby out of her belly. You want to know why I called myself after those retched fool Journeymen. You want to know…"

Dar's pacing had taken him away from the pair, and he had his back just slightly turned when he heard the sound of two blades being drawn. By the time he turned to face them, it was over.

Letin's head fell to the ground some distance from his body. The body then slumped over and poured blood all over

Bounce's body. Yspeida looked at the headless torso and put the swords away.

"You were wrong, sorcerer. All I wanted to know is that you're dead."

THIRTEEN

What You Are

And when the tears fall, will you find the
Master. When blood spills, the seas boil, and all
nightmares are real, the Master will be there.
—chapter 10, verse 57, the Book of Truth

Adalia sat in the center of town and wept. Drij knew why
she cried. She cried for herself, she cried for her baby,
and she cried for every dead soul that called Redemption
home. So she let it all out, barely noticing the small crowd of
people gathered around her. Drij stood over her, guarding her,
but not wanting to comfort her for fear of crying himself. His
loss was right at the surface as well, and serving as her guard
kept it in check. But the crowd was getting larger.

"Miss Adalia." Drij had his back to her—in part to avoid
seeing her tears, but mostly to keep the crowd in front of him.
"I believe we need to find a more private location."

Adalia stood. "Lead the way." When he turned to face her,
he could see that her tears had slowed but not abated.

Drij looked around. "This way." He gently took her hand and led her toward the Church of the Holy. He hoped it would be empty now that Vulia had been exposed.

"Do you think Dar is going to die?" She stumbled and surely would have fallen if she hadn't been holding his hand. As it was, she ended up on one knee, her hair falling into her face.

Drij turned and brushed her hair from her eyes. She almost looked like his eldest daughter. "I have a feeling that he has been through the worst and survived it. He knows when to stand and when to fade. If he could not best them, he would have come here to us." He helped her up and started toward the church again.

"Why is there suffering?" He could hear that she had started crying again.

"Why is there anything?" He pulled at her hand to keep her moving.

The continued in silence until they got to the church. Peering inside, Drij was glad to see it was empty. He gently sat her down in a corner of the main room. Adalia collapsed to the floor and resumed her outpouring of emotion. Wanting to give her some privacy, Drij contemplated his next move. He asked himself, what would Dar do? He studied the room, paying attention to Adalia's location. While the corner offered protection on two sides, she was barely defended from the front. To address this, Drij moved a few pews around her, fortifying her position, until he felt she was safe. Once finished, he turned to her and found her sleeping. He took the hint and quietly made his way over to the entrance of his fortifications and awaited her return to consciousness.

Dar and Yspeida walked silently toward town, Dar in front, Yspeida trailing. Dar had abandoned the search for the trap door the dwarves had dug. In the chaos after the battle he couldn't locate it, and after Drij and Adalia went through it, he figured the dwarves might have sealed the shaft. The walk would do them both good. As long as the silence held.

"I had to do it," Yspeida said softly.

"I don't care." Dar kept his eyes forward. "Where I come from, you don't slaughter unarmed people."

"No matter how evil and vile they are."

"No matter." Dar thought about turning to face her, but that would be taken as a challenge. He wanted to mentor her, and raising her defenses wouldn't help. "The rules don't change if the combatant is evil. You live by your rules at all times, or before long you'll be making enough exceptions that you won't have any rules worth upholding."

She erupted in anger on him. "What if it was your family? What if he had defiled your kin?"

"He did," Dar said softly.

Yspeida stopped. Dar noticed the lack of her footfalls but kept moving, albeit a little slower.

"Letin called out the name of the Journeymen," he continued. "He sullied their name. He defiled all they stand for, made an enemy where there had only been friendship."

Yspeida started walking again, with a quick trot to close the gap. "Why do you care about these Journeymen?" she asked.

He didn't look at her. "Because I am one of them."

Dar could hear the anger turn to frustration. He wondered what her expression was right now, but figured eye contact wouldn't be a good idea. "And you let me ramble on about killing them. You knew at some point I would figure it out and come after you."

"I had hoped it wouldn't come to that."

"And if it had?"

"I would have defended myself." Dar stopped and turned to her. "But I would not have killed you. I knew your anger was misdirected. I knew you really didn't mean the brotherhood any harm. The vile creature that destroyed your kin was not a member; I knew that as soon as your story was told."

"What is it like, living in a world where you know everything?" She was talking with her hands, her face turning red in either anger or embarrassment.

Dar couldn't help himself and laughed. "It gets a little boring." Yspeida wasn't laughing, though. He could tell that she was starting to shift from frustration to rage. "Let me tell you another story."

He sat on the hard, bare soil and motioned for her to do the same. She continued to stand. And look down on him, he noticed.

"I was recruited into the Journeymen after a period of great upheaval in my life. I was drawn to them because of what they stood for, what they believed in, and the good deeds that they did all over this land." He looked up at her. "That was over three years ago."

"Three...?" She sat down next to him. "I thought you were a long-standing, skilled ranger, at this for over a decade."

"My journey toward the fellowship of the Journeyman is a long and sordid tale, but when I saw the truth, I knew I was where I belonged."

"What have you done? Where have you gone?"

"The training is amazing. I travelled with my first mentor Katowyn for a while, but there was…" He paused, hoping she didn't notice him blushing. "A complication, so she and I parted ways. Staying friends, of course. I have been to your homeland, fought in the last great siege around Eagles Glen, travelled around the Chaotic Disunion, and much, much more."

"Interesting stories, my friend."

Both Yspeida and Dar looked up. It was Gryphilix. He landed gently and helped them both to their feet.

"But I would rather hear the tale of how you two ended up here, why there is a man missing his head, a wall only a couple of inches tall, and burn marks all over the forest. And let's start with why my steward Bounce is dead."

Dar placed his arm on Gryphilix's shoulder. "Bounce betrayed us and was slain by the headless man."

"Betrayed?" Gryphilix started walking toward the town.

Yspeida chimed in. "He was working for the evil magic user Letin and his sister Vulia."

"Let us go to the coach wagon." Gryphilix started to pick up the pace. "It's just a little bit over here."

They were in sight of the coach wagon when Gryphilix started up again. "Why did the headless man kill him?"

"His name was Letin. He had his reasons." Dar left it at that.

"Who cut off the head of the other dead man?"

The silence hung in the air for a motion before Dar answered. "I have no idea."

"Knock?" Yspeida called. "Where are you, Knock?"

"I'm over here." Dar could see her now. It was clear that she'd yelled as loud as she could, but it came out just above a whisper. The driver's seat was once again occupied by Gryphilix—as Dar climbed aboard, he could see him start to move the drive lever.

Dar crossed the floor of the coach wagon to her side, with Yspeida right beside him.

"Dar!" Knock said.

"Hello, old friend." Dar smiled at her. "How bad is it?"

"I've been through worse." She tried to sit up. "But not much. Remember Gulch?"

Dar put his hands on her, and she closed her eyes. He touched her as gently as he could, but any pressure made her wince.

"Broken ribs." Dar whispered as he moved his hands to her belly. It felt bloated. Again, any touch made tears form at the corner of her eyes. "Ruptured something," he said.

"Tell me something"—she paused to take a breath—"I don't already know."

"Some of these wounds have already started to set, and some have already started to fester."

"I understand." Knock closed her eyes.

"I don't understand." Yspeida turned to Dar. "What does it mean?"

Dar looked Yspeida in the eye. "I can use my magic to get her out of danger and heal her internal wounds, but the bones have started to set. My magic will seal them in whichever way they have already started to heal. If they are wrong…"

"I will be crippled or disabled in one way or another." Knock put her hand on Dar's hand. "I understand. Please do it."

The coach wagon started to move, and Dar reached out to stabilize her body. He adjusted her on the floor, trying to get her into a comfortable position, then looked at Yspeida. "Hold her. She will need assistance until I can cast my spell."

Yspeida looked down at Dar's patient. "I'm here for you, Knock."

"Yspeida, dear." She smiled weakly. "You've been a good friend."

Dar started a chant and rubbed his hands together. He would use his most powerful spell, Cure Critical Wounds. If he had access to a full Heal spell, it would correct the broken bones and undo all the other damage, but only those of pure clerical power could gain enough favor from the gods to perform such powerful actions. He finished the casting and placed his hands on Knock. The spell power penetrated her body, and Dar knew what was happening: Knock was feeling the tingle of the magic as it worked to undo the damage the daemons had caused. The stiffness in her chest would go away; the tenderness of her abdomen would fade. He'd had this spell cast on him many a time. She took a deep breath, and Dar could see that it was without pain. - Judging by the joy in her eyes, it was for the first time in what seemed like forever. Even the jostling and the rocking of the coach wagon as it picked up speed caused her no visible distress. As the tingle started to fade, her body's natural healing powers kicked in double time and she struggled to keep awake.

Dar was weak too, and as he pulled away from her, he softly caressed her head. "We'll see you in a bit, sleepy one."

Knock closed her eyes and was asleep before he could even try to stand.

"You're tired too, Dar." Yspeida helped him to his feet.

"Well said," Gryphilix called out from the driver's seat. "The she-warrior and I can keep an eye on things while you get some rest."

Dar looked at Yspeida. She nodded.

"I will rest."

When Dar woke up, the coach wagon was in Redemption.

Drij heard the commotion outside and decided to investigate. He had been standing guard over Adalia for over half a day, and she was still sleeping. The sun was starting to cross the horizon beyond the Heaven Spire when he emerged from the church, and his joints were stiff all over. He quickly made his way out into the yard in front of the church. Across the commons he saw the back end of the coach wagon, and he could see Dar and Yspeida climbing down the steps in the back. He didn't see Bounce or Gryphilix but assumed they were there. He waved his arms, hoping to catch Dar's eye. Yspeida saw him and pointed him out to Dar. Then the pair started over to the church.

"Well met!" Drij called out when they were within earshot.

"Where is Adalia?" Dar called out, starting into a trot.

"She is inside, resting. How did the battle go?" Drij led them inside toward the resting spot of Adalia.

"It went." Dar was clearly focused on Adalia.

"Bounce was killed," Yspeida said somberly. "But he betrayed us."

Some of the joy came out of Drij's heart. "What of the two evils?"

"The man was slain," Dar said. They had reached Drij's fortifications—Dar worked his way around them until he could see Adalia resting and then turned back to Drij. "But the woman, Vulia, escaped. She might be returning to this temple."

"I doubt that." Drij looked around the temple area. "They won't let her return here."

"They?" Yspeida looked around.

"The walls have ears." Dar was focused on Drij. "How are you?"

"I am fine." He had done a lot of thinking and meditating while Adalia slept. "I am truly fine."

Dar nodded. "Then what is next?"

"We get May and set her free in the Lake of Tears." Adalia's voice swept over them.

Everyone turned. Dar's face erupted into a smile when his eyes met hers. She smiled weakly, still drowsy.

Dar walked over and reached out for her hand and started to help her up. As she rose to her feet, she kept going beyond vertical and crashed into him in an awkward hug. They clung to each other for a moment and then suddenly pushed away, as if remembering the others in the room.

She reached down and straightened her clothes. "I'm ready to finish my journey. We need May."

Dar turned to Drij. "Can I have the Closet of Xio, please?"

On the Ethereal plane, the shadowy outline of the most powerful magic user ever to darken Holimoren stood from his position of repose and started to prepare for the moment. The moment that would give him access to the living world. The moment that would let him out of this prison without walls and allow him to unleash his vision on the world again. He was ready. He paused and tilted his head.

Were they ready for him?

Dar held the tiny door in the palm of his hand. "Yspeida, guard the opening to our little pew fort, if you don't mind."

Yspeida nodded. She pulled Hack and Slash from their sheaths and stood between the church's front door and the opening of the area Drij had barricaded with pews. Drij turned to face where Dar was placing the smaller door on the ground. Dar uttered the magic words, and the door became as large as a normal door, some seven feet tall. Adalia came to Dar's side, and Drij flanked him on the other. Dar reached out and grabbed the handle.

He gave it a turn.

The blinding glow of transdimensional energy crossed from the Prime Material plane to the plane of Ether. It formed a tunnel between the magic door and the other-reality space that was the Closet of Xio. As the door cracked open, it opened for a moment into the Ether, right at the feet of the shadowy figure.

He stepped into the light.

Dar cracked open the door, finding it brighter than normal inside. He stepped in, with Drij right behind him, but no sooner had he crossed the threshold than he felt a draft. A wisp of smoke flew past his head and landed on the ground about six hand widths from the back wall of the closet. The smoke turned into a skeleton. The skeleton had fiery red eyes and wore tattered clothes, though it possessed no more than clumps of skin—some with hair—on the top of the skull. But as the moments passed, the smoke began to billow on the bones, turning into flesh. The skeleton took a deep breath, and its body started to regenerate.

Dar, based on his training in the magic arts, could tell the creature was recharging its magic power. The plane of Magic didn't flow through the Ethereal plane, so long had it been denied access to the magic energies. With each passing moment in this reality, it was gaining power. The skeleton began to wave its hands, even as the flesh rebuilt around them. The power transfer was not complete, yet it was obviously starting to cast a spell: Wizard Lock. Usually used to keep a door shut, it really just held a door wherever it was. The Master wanted out, and the way back was this open door. It had to remain open for him, at all costs.

Dar knew the door would remain open until he could dispel the magic—he wanted nothing more than to close the door and seal off this monster. Dar reached for the hilt of his sword and drew Winter from its sheath. But the skeleton was a step ahead. It must have had decades to plan this moment, and as far as Dar could tell, its plan was going as well as it could have hoped. Fog formed at the door and rolled inward from it, accumulating on the man, now no longer just a skeleton. He drew in the flow of the magic from outside the closet and shed some of it in a blinding flash. The energy from the discharge tossed Dar and his friends about. Dar hit the wall next to the door, and Drij did the same on the other side. Yspeida and Adalia were blasted out the door and free of the closet—Yspeida hit one of the pews, and Adalia landed beside her.

"It must not be allowed out of the closet!" Dar yelled over the reverberating thunder of the discharge.

He wasn't sure if anybody heard him, but suddenly it was silent. The skeleton was now fully clothed, a man at all but full strength, and he stood at the far end of the closet, ready for action. His hair was red, almost as red as the center of his eyes, and he had hair that looked like the mane of a lion, long and flowing. He was fairly well muscled and had a strong chin.

When he spoke, it boomed and filled the closet. "My name is Kygger. But I doubt your history remembers me at all."

"The Master?" Drij blurted out. "The one the Book of Truth is about?"

"And the cause of Armageddon," Dar observed.

The Master laughed the way a parent laughs at the folly of the child. "The very same."

"But the Book of Truth tells that the war was hundreds of years ago." Drij looked over at Dar, who remained silent.

Kygger smiled and ran his fingers through his hair. "But a blink of an eye for me. You see, I have been imprisoned on the Ethereal plane. Nice place, though just a tiny bit boring."

"How have you cheated death?" Drij started to struggle to his feet.

"Cheated?" The Master's cold laugh echoed for a moment, but then he turned ominously serious. "My dear boy, you forget who you are talking to. I *am* Death."

Dar sprung to his feet, pulled Winter out, and lunged at Kygger. The sword crackled though the air as its cold power sprung to full force. The Master dodged slightly, and the blow just grazed him.

Dar had expected the frost power of the blade to freeze his foe. No such event had occurred—in fact, Dar could almost feel cold coming from the Master. The ancient sorcerer reached back with his left hand and slapped Dar across the face. Cold permeated Dar's skin, and his mind fogged up as the blow sent him back against the wall beside the entrance.

"For centuries I have awaited the chance to return to the living world. The plane of Ether, it isn't really alive. Only by the sheer force of my own will did I survive. But it changed me. I have foreseen every moment, and your toys won't hurt me. I've been watching your world from the Near Ethereal for years. I watch all, all the time. I know your weaknesses, your favorite methods, the powers of your weapons. I know everything."

Drij was on his feet, but before he could make a move, Yspeida flashed by him, running in from outside. She swung Hack and Slash at the Master, who dodged the first blow. The second hit him strong, right under the left arm, but the blade didn't penetrate; it just cut the cloth of his robe and stopped when it hit the skin of the horrid man. Again the Master replied with blow, and this one sent Yspeida flying back out the door. Dar knew that she wasn't sheltered from the cold and paralysis of the Master's touch the way Winter had sheltered him, though—by the time her body landed (by the sound of it, some two strides from the wall), she would already have blacked out.

Kygger smirked at Dar, his eyes showing how much he enjoyed dealing with Yspeida. "I haven't even used any of my most powerful spells against you, and you're already half defeated."

Drij took the moment to cast a spell of his own. Dar recognized it as Protection from Evil, which would create a small area where the evil, destructive energy of the Master could not travel—and best yet, he was casting it in the doorway of the closet. As long as the spell held, Kygger and his destruction could not get out.

"You think that will stop me?" The Master raised his hands and performed a quick spell. Flames jumped from his fingertips and fanned out, covering the whole wall that contained the door. The flames hit Drij's skin, threatening to burn him horribly, but died as fast as they arrived, thanks to the protection afforded by Winter. Dar had just regained his footing when the flames hit him and likewise extinguished.

"You know," the Master said, "I have forgotten how good it feels to be alive. There is little magic power on the Ethereal plane. Well, none, except what you bring with you. This doorway has allowed a flood of it to enter my veins, to fill my soul. And since I used the last of my power at…" He chuckled. "Well, you know…I have been without my spells for centuries. Only little cantrips have I had. The sleight-of-hand stuff and the minor magicks like how to repair a lost button or clean your hair, even as it falls out."

The Master paused his rant to unleash another spell, and this time, magic arrows flew out of his hands. They struck Dar head on, though his armor took most of the beating. Punch after punch of the arrows struck him and knocked the wind right out of him. Having been pounded back against the wall, he fell slightly askew, partially out in the doorway. Drij grabbed him by the scruff of the neck and dragged him outside into the pew area. Then he turned and faced the evil that was now walking out of the closet toward them. The Master stopped at the edge of the Protection from Evil spell; he could see out of the closet but couldn't yet escape it.

"Adalia has been key to my success. I had thought about making that Vulia my queen for her loyalty, but Adalia has been the true champion for me." The Master stopped to look back into the closet, apparently to see if there was anything that he could use in the days ahead. "You see, Letin put a touch of the Oil of Etherealness on the back of Adalia's neck while she was under his spell. I could see that patch as easily as you can see the sun at high noon. I followed it. I knew sometime soon she would come here, and as soon as the gate to the area opened, I would have my revenge."

The Master went to the far back and opened one of the small chests on a shelf about chest high. He dug around inside for a moment. "Pretty low-key stuff here. Curatives, poison treatments, pretty mundane articles for such a wondrous piece of work as the famed Closest of Xio." He shut the lid. "Perhaps I will make Vulia my queen, and Adalia can be my favored concubine. Fancy a life as a whore, my love?" He feigned shock. "That's right, you already are one." He opened the chest that contained May and pulled out her lifeless body. He held it up like a rag doll. He showed Adalia her dead child. "How did that work out for you? I found the whole episode quite entertaining."

At that, Adalia snapped, and she charged at Kygger. Drij tried to stop her, but the Master succeeded where he had failed. He cast Levitation on her and held her aloft just outside the closet door by pure thought.

"I can't have you damaging my property. I need all your parts in good shape for what I have in mind."

He walked toward the door, May in one hand, the other outstretched, guiding the spell energy. "You see, Letin was just learning the fun that the female form can provide. I learned a long time ago what I like, and I have had a long time to figure out all the things I want to do. It might hurt." He laughed. "It will hurt a lot, but it won't kill you. You won't die until I've had my fill of you. Then I will have Vulia and all the other tasty morsels of womanhood that cover this fair land. My appetite knows no bounds."

Dar struggled to his feet again and tried a spell—a stroke of lightning shot from his finger, and the bolt arced out toward the Master. This caused the Master to drop the hand that was holding Adalia up as he used it to absorb the power of Dar's electricity, which covered his arm in blue sparks that faded into his skin. Adalia fell from the air and hit the slate floor with a thud. She would be winded, Dar knew, but it did not sound like anything was broken.

"I grow tired of this game; I'm coming out into *my* world."

Kygger uttered one of the seven power-word spells, and Drij and Adalia joined Yspeida in sudden slumber. Only Dar remained awake.

The Master summoned his strength and cast another spell. Dar immediately knew it to be Dispel Magic. He needed to stop the Master, but he was too far away. The Master finished the spell, and the magic runes from Drij's Protection spell faded away.

Suddenly Dar heard another spell being started—this time from outside the closet. He heard the incantation and knew who was casting the spell.

"Go, Knock!" Dar yelled. "Lock him in!" He turned and saw Knock, who stood near the front door of the church, finishing the Anti-Magic Shell spell, which would lock the magic power of the Master in the closet. The anti-magic shell also cancelled the Master's Wizard Lock spell. The door to the Closet of Xio was now magic free. He could be sealed in.

Kygger let fly with a lightning bolt of his own. But it never made it past the doorway, as it dissipated in the anti-magic field—apparently, he'd only heard part of the magic phrase Knock had spoken. Kygger then went up to the doorway and reached out with his hand. A cascading green glow met his flesh and caused him to step back in pain. The expression on his face told Dar that he hadn't felt anything for a long time.

Dar smiled and put Winter away. This was now a job for Weeper. He pulled an arrow from his magic quiver and let it fly through the door. Kygger, focused on his hand, didn't see it coming, but it didn't matter. It hit the anti-magic shell and exploded.

"Magic arrows? My boy, this is quite the standoff we have. Your magic can't get in, and mine can't get out. I can wait another dozen lifetimes for this to play out. Can you?"

Dar knew that sooner or later Kygger would figure a way out of the trap. And Knock's anti-magic shell wouldn't last much more than an hour.

"What are our options?" Knock inquired from behind him.

"Yes, what are our options?" The Master mocked her from inside the closet.

"There is only one option." Dar studied the inside of the closet. Timing would be key. He closed his eyes and readied his spell. He opened his eyes and looked back at Knock. "On my command, I need you to drop the anti-magic shell."

"But…" Knock started.

"Excellent idea, my boy," finished Kygger.

"This will work, but you'll have to trust me. I can't talk about it with him"—Dar pointed at the Master, who was now pacing the closet—"around."

"Okay." Knock's tone told Dar that she had a great deal of doubt about his plan.

Kygger closed his eyes, no doubt to focus on his spell list and ready his thoughts.

But as soon as they were shut, Dar pulled out one of his fat-bodied arrows and let it fly. The arrow, powered by technology instead of magic, flew through the shell without incident, and by the time Kygger heard the roar of the chemical reaction, it was too late. The arrow struck him straight in the center of his chest, knocking May out of his hands to just inside the entrance and causing him to fly back against the far wall. Chests fell from the shelves, slowing Kygger down further. The room filled with the smoke from the arrow, and chemicals exploded everywhere when it impacted the back wall.

Dar dropped Weeper and ran toward the room. "Now!" he yelled. He could feel the shell drop as he passed through the portal. He grabbed May and turned to run back out of the small room. The flames had begun to consume everything flammable in the space, and smoke made it impossible to see. Dar leaped out of the door and kicked it shut with his foot.

Dar tossed the body of the baby to Knock, who was so stunned to see it coming at her that she almost dropped it. With his hands now free, Dar cast a spell at the door in record time. And then he watched.

Inside the closet, the smoke and fire just made Kygger even madder. The arrow didn't do any damage to him, as the magic of the Ether made him immune to normal weapons. But it didn't make him immune to the laws of physics. He stood up, having been blasted to the back of the room, and tried to determine the cause of the fire. But everything was burning.

He walked over to the door and reached out for the handle. But as his hand met the metal, the metal disappeared.

"You cast Disintegrate on the doorway?" Knock looked up from tending to the wounded Drij, Yspeida, and Adalia.

"It needed to be done." Dar removed his armor and grimaced at the fist-sized bruises that had formed where the magic missiles had impacted. "You know they are going to be fine. As a power word, Stun doesn't kill."

"That doesn't mean you should ignore the plight of the less fortunate." Knock looked at him sternly.

Dar just stared at where the doorway had been. He wondered, just for a moment, what had happened to Kygger, then he turned to help his friends.

Kygger felt every moment of time passing as the room and the reality it connected him to evaporate from around him. All the magic items, all the gold, all of it lost all density and floated off into the air, into the Ether. He wasn't screaming from the pain—he welcomed that. He was screaming because he had been so close, only to fall short again. Then he wondered for a moment, was it *again* again? As his body returned to the form that he had spent the last hundred years in, he knew he didn't have to keep track of his attempts.

One would succeed.

And the world would be his.

FOURTEEN

Journeyman

You may reach your destination, but it is rarely
the end of the journey.
—Gramal Kilshan, Journeyman

When everyone in the group had finally regained their
senses, it was closer to dawn than dusk. Adalia, lacking
the training and resistance that battling had provided the rest,
was the last to do so. When she finally opened her eyes, she
noticed that everything was very different from when she'd
lost consciousness.

She was still in the Church of the Holy, but the pew fortress that Drij had constructed was missing. She was lying on
top of a pew, with blankets and a pillow underneath her. It
was homey and comfortable and not at all like she remembered this place to be. She sat up and looked around. The
sight of Drij at the far end sweeping the floor brought her an
immediate sense of calm. Until she realized that no one else
was around.

"Where is everyone?" she said, a little too loud for the hour.

"Shhh." Drij walked toward her and then stopped, leaning the broom against one of the pews. "You've had a busy day."

"Where is Dar?" Panic set into her voice. "Where is May?"

Drij reached where she was lying just as she swung her legs out, preparing to stand. "They are together, lass. He is preparing her for the last part of her journey."

"She's ready," Dar said as he walked in, holding a cedar panel that he had ripped from the wall. On top was the lifeless body of May, in a beautiful white dress that extended past her legs by about a quarter of an arm's length. Her hair was tended to and braided, and only her pale complexion indicated that she wasn't just a babe sleeping. Looking at her, Adalia tried to remain strong. Her child was so beautiful that she just wanted her to sit up or wiggle or do anything. She wanted her to be a baby again instead a body.

But she never would be.

"If we leave now, we can be at the Lake of Tears before midday." Drij rubbed her hand.

Dar set the board with May's body on top down next to Adalia. Then he reached out and touched Adalia's check. "We will all help her on her way."

Adalia could only nod. Drij stayed with her as Dar went back into one of the small rooms off of the main chapel and came out with Yspeida and Knock. Yspeida had a cloak in hand, and she wrapped it around Adalia as she stood up.

The group was still walking when the dawn came. They were close to the site of the previous day's battle, but there were no bodies, just circling birds. Dar paid it no mind, as they worked across the grassless hardtack and small stones toward their goal. They had continued on for just a little while when the form of Gryphilix appeared in the skies above them. Dar kept walking, and Gryphilix landed next to him and kept pace.

"I buried Bounce," he said. "I figured somebody should help him toward forgiveness."

Dar looked over at him. "Was the headless body still there when you arrived?"

"No."

"Interesting," Drij commented from back in the ranks.

"I saw no burn marks, no drag marks." Gryphilix looked forward the whole time. Dar thought he saw tears in the corner of his eyes. "Whatever force took the wizard left Bounce alone. Actually cleaned him up a little, I would think."

"Vulia." Dar returned his focus to the trail ahead.

"That's my guess. So watch out, she's probably still in the area." Gryphilix kept his eyes on the horizon.

"And that's why you're here."

"I'll keep you covered up top, but my sleeping time draws near, so don't journey too far."

Dar frowned. "We are just headed to the Lake of Tears."

Gryphilix turned and looked at Adalia. When he saw that she was carrying a baby instead of the familiar box, his tears seemed to well up again. He focused ahead once more.

"After you reach the lake, I will return to Redemption. I need to find a new helper." As Gryphilix finished his sentence, he returned to the air.

"Understood." Dar said it loud enough to be heard by Gryphilix as he flew away.

Vulia sat next to the fireplace in their retreat in the forest. She held her brother's head in one hand and a bottle of whiskey in the other. She took a long draw from the bottle and closed her eyes as the hard spirits burned all the way down. It was a cheap bottle, but it wasn't the flavor she was after. She didn't want taste, she wanted not to remember—she wanted not to feel any more.

After the mouthful reached her stomach, she contemplated the head. She held it by the hair; the face was without any expression. She knew death had come quickly, and deep within her, she was both glad and sad that it had been that way. He was her brother, but he had been so vile, even for her. They shared so many adventures, but he had become abusive. She didn't like what she had become with him around. She had enjoyed the Holy, and she had enjoyed some of the other men. But he had taken so much from her.

She knew she could take his head and have him resurrected—or she could throw his head into the fire and find her own way to the Master.

Another draw from the bottle helped to clear things up.

She put Letin's head down on the edge of the fireplace and leaned back, allowing her hair to dangle free as she stood up. She became a little dizzy—she had drunk more tonight than she ever remembered having. She put her foot next to the head to stabilize herself. Her foot touched the head.

And pushed it in.

She would find her own destiny.

The four stood around Adalia as the shore of the Lake of Tears glistened in the late-morning sun. She was crouched near the edge, her arms outstretched, with May just above the water. Adalia started to pitch forward, but Dar leaped forward, grabbed her around the waist, and steadied her. She looked back at him and smiled. They didn't want to find out what would happen should she fall in.

Drij approached the water and opened his arms wide. "Oh gods of the beautiful land of Holimoren, your offspring and followers here at the lakeside bask in your glory. We ask you to take this child into your fold and make her in the afterlife what she couldn't be in life. Forgive us for our sins and allow this vessel of purity and beauty to join in your holy presence."

Adalia let May go, and the baby fell the six inches to the water's surface. But there was no splash, and the body didn't dip under the water. It just slowly drifted to the center of the lake.

Adalia stood, backing away from the edge, and watched. Dar put his arm around her. Drij kept his arms open, hoping to gain favor for the babe. Yspeida and Knock stood next to each other, looking unsure of what was supposed to be happening.

Slowly May started to sink—Adalia could hardly bear to see her go. But just as the body sunk halfway under the water, it appeared that invisible arms took hold of it and lifted it up.

May started to rise out of the water.

As she floated into the sky, a bright light rose out of the water. Knock and Yspeida couldn't look at the glow, and they looked away. Dar did his best, but it was just too bright.

In the end, only Drij and Adalia could see what was happening.

A thin woman of pure light held May up to her chest and started walking toward them where they stood on the lakeshore.

"Adalia, mother of May. You have suffered a great deal at the hands of evil; your wish for May will be granted."

The light shone enough to make Adalia blink her for several seconds. When her eyes adjusted, the woman of light was still there, but May was no longer in her arms.

That's when she noticed that a child of maybe six years with gossamer wings flew nearby the goddess's head, which was now just a few feet away. Her wings were golden, her hair a perfect blond. Her eyes were blue, but the pupils were missing. She was naked—the dress not needed where she was headed—and the color of her skin was now a slight bronze. A smile crossed May's face as she reached out to Adalia and handed her the dress she had made May from a sheet.

"Until we meet again, Mother." May's voice was made of the wind and soft as the down of a baby duck. "I love you."

Adalia reached out, tears streaming down her face. She took the garment. "I love you too, May."

May smiled again. Adalia watched as her child returned to the woman made of light.

The Goddess of Forgiveness turned to Drij. "Drij, your soul will never be completely clean, but rest assured that you have earned your redemption. Share what you have learned, and perhaps you will wash away more of the stain."

"I understand, your holiness." Drij lowered his head in appreciation.

With that, the goddess and May both smiled at Adalia. Floating effortlessly above the water, they turned away from the lakeshore and walked on the air back out into the center of the lake.

Suddenly, there was a flash and they were gone.

"What happened?" Yspeida said, blinking and squinting as she scanned the area.

"Happily, May is an angel, I may yet get into the Heavens, and I know what I must do," Drij said without emotion. He turned and started toward Redemption, not waiting for Dar or the rest of them.

"Forever starts today," he called out to the rest of them. "And fate is awaiting all of us in Redemption."

It was just about suppertime when they reached the town. Gryphilix had moved the coach wagon around behind the church, and the smoke rising from the chimney suggested that the fire burning inside had probably been started by his hand.

They went inside to find Gryphilix eating a bowl of stew between yawns.

Dar and Adalia walked together to the front of the main chamber, stopping just short of the altar. Adalia looked at May's dress, not knowing what to do with it. Dar felt pained but had no idea what to say.

Drij looked at the pair of them. "Let's place her dress on top of the old altar. Maybe she will bring a blessing to this house and allow it to become a place of healing and joy."

Adalia nodded.

Dar ripped a board of red cedar from one of the pews that had been broken in the battle with Kygger and walked to the front of the room. He placed it gently on the altar, and

Adalia set the dress on top of it. Drij walked down the aisle toward the offering.

"Food is ready." Knock stood by the door to the living quarters of the church.

"Thanks, Knock." Drij held out his hand and took Adalia's. Dar took her other hand and helped her past the dress in repose and into the living chambers.

The smell of stew, probably venison, filled the room. The potatoes and carrots were a bit smallish, but the group was hungry, so it didn't matter. Each took a bowl and helped themselves. Yspeida took the largest bowl and started to gulp it down, clearly used to eating on the run. Knock had left drinks at each table setting. Being a church of greed and evil, all the cups were gold goblets.

"I have decided to stay," Drij announced.

"In what fashion?" Dar asked, fearing the worst.

Drij set his spoon to the lip of the bowl and looked each at the table in the eye in turn. "I came to this town to make my peace and then leave this world. What happened along the way, and especially what happened at the lake, has shown to me that I must do better with my life and help those most in need. I will rebuild this church into the assistance and healing reprieve it was intended to be. I will teach the ways of the True Gods, and hopefully someday I will join May in the Heavens."

Dar took his goblet and held it aloft in toast. "To Father Drij, Father to Redemption!"

They all in turn held up their cups and drank deeply.

Gryphilix smiled. "Great. You can guard my body while I sleep then, Father. I...." He yawned for what seemed to Dar far too long a period. "I won't make it another dawn without entering my sleeping phase."

"I will be your helper," Yspeida called out as he began to walk away. "My mission is also complete, and I need a new purpose."

All of them smiled. Gryphilix looked beside himself with joy. "You'll make a great hand. Welcome aboard, she-warrior."

Yspeida looked at Dar. "I will join him on one condition: that you will start to teach me the ways of the Journeymen while he sleeps."

Dar's mouth was full, so he just shook his head.

"What?" Yspeida looked stunned. "Why not?"

"The training must be conducted by an elder," Dar said, his cheek still filled with venison. A smile crossed his face as he waited.

"That would be me." Knock took a sip from her goblet and grinned.

"You too, Knock?" Yspeida turned and looked at her friend.

"I trained Dar, and I will train you. Besides, he is no longer a student—he doesn't need me. He's a full Journeyman now." She toasted Dar with her glass. "I need to slow down for a while anyway."

"I will start an orphanage in my hometown and be a mother to those without," Adalia stated. "Once I get back home." She cast a shy glance at Dar.

Drij looked at his former hireling. "What will you do now, Master Dar?"

Dar grinned. "Sounds like I have been offered another guide job."

AUTHOR'S NOTES

I wrote the background story of this novel before the passing of my wife's nephew Brandon at the age of five months. May is a focal point of the story, and though I worried that including her might cause further pain, I felt I could not change the story and take her out. So I honor him with her story.

I would like to thank the usual people who helped behind the scenes with this text: my father and mother; my wife, Nikki; my wonderful kids, Devon and Lorna; my fellow writing buddies at NaNo, especially the great Niki Maki; the book club that helped me push myself toward this plot and characters; my iPod shuffle for giving me that perfect set of tunes to keep me typing; my friends Stuart, Susan, Vinnie, Jeff, Matt, Jeff, and Jeremy; and Chris N. and everyone who reads this for taking the time to do so. For the record, I finished the first draft of this on December 20, 2005. Fiction takes time.

Special thanks to my Aunt Jean, the Jean the Great from the epigraph of Chapter Four: "Needs must." A fitting expression that I use a lot.

D Dean Boom